"*Death Valley Blooms* expertly toes the line between hopelessness and tenderness, between the horrors of what is to come and the small joys of today. Centering familial relationships, this novella explores everything we pass down: curses, love, and everything in between."
—A.D. Sui, author of *The Dragonfly Gambit*

"*Death Valley Blooms* is a breathtaking, atmospheric novella that explores hard-hitting topics such as gendered inheritance, mourning, and sacrifice with an impressively light touch. S.M. Mack's writing is full of humor and sobriety, which held my attention from start to finish. If you enjoy stories that bridge meditative, slice-of-life scenes with fast-paced action, this book will not disappoint."
— Liza Wemakor, author of *Loving Safoa*

"This is a gorgeous novella from an important new talent—sharp, lyrical, and deeply honest about family relationships. Read S.M. Mack now, before everyone else discovers her work."
—Theodora Goss, author of *The Thorn and the Blossom*

Neon Hemlock Press
www.neonhemlock.com
@neonhemlock

Death Valley Blooms
S.M. Mack

Cover Illustration by Rose Mayer
Interior Design and Layout by dave ring
Edited by dave ring

Print ISBN-13: 978-1-966503-12-5
Ebook ISBN-13: 978-1-966503-13-2

S.M. Mack
DEATH VALLEY BLOOMS
Neon Hemlock Press

NEON HEMLOCK

DEATH VALLEY BLOOMS

S.M. MACK

To my parents.

None of this would have happened without you.
Love you both.

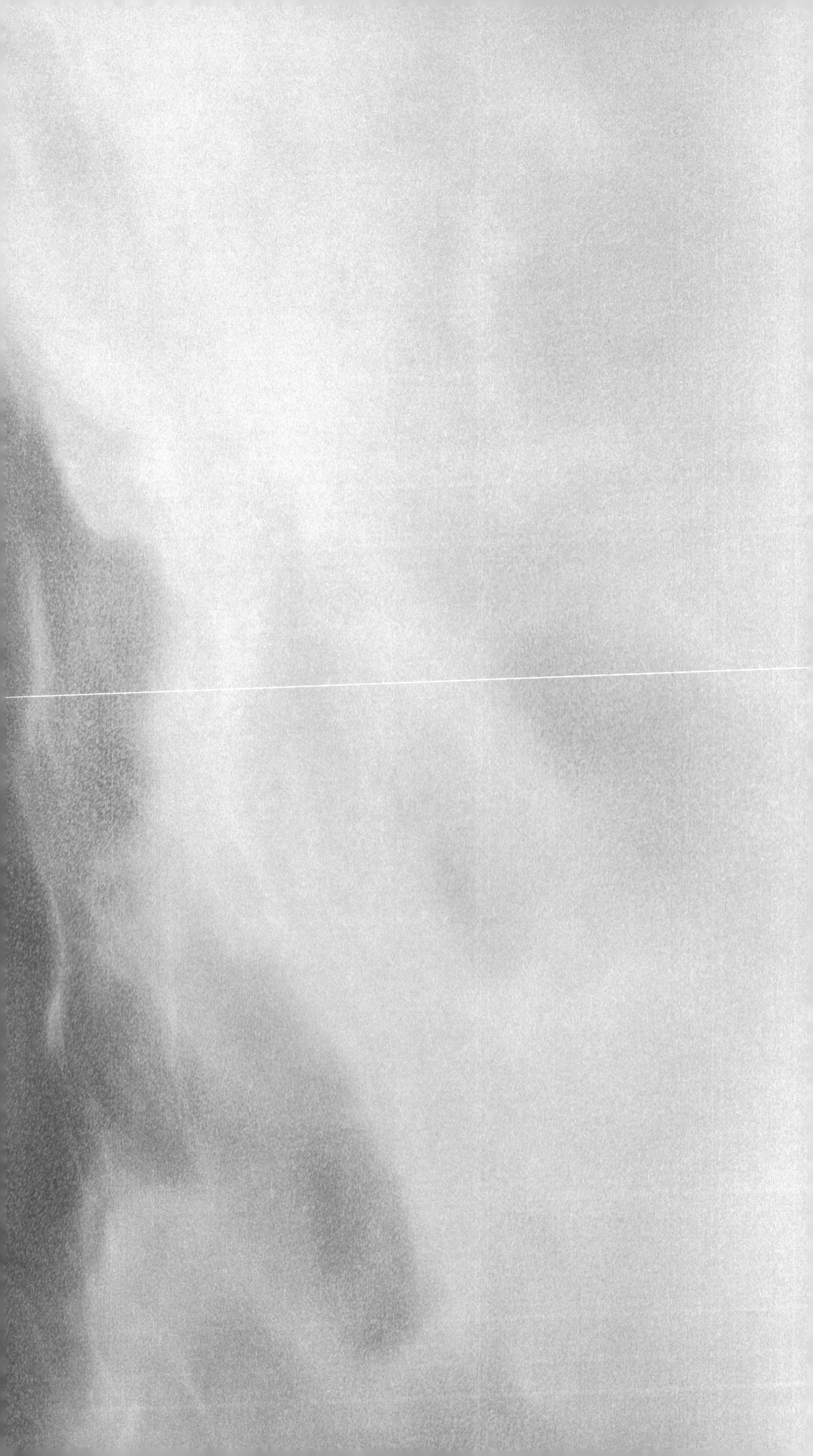

I.

WHEN DEATH VALLEY called Mom, I drove her out by myself. When she shouted, "Here! Stop here," I jerked the wheel to the right and tried to remember to breathe as we dropped off the asphalt with a bounce. In her haste, she left the door open and skinned her knee on the edge of the pavement.

I threw myself out of the driver's seat and raced after her. She'd already risen and started running, but back then I ran cross country. Even winded from yelling, I caught up, grabbed her shoulder, and tried to spin her around. She jerked against my grip and we tumbled to the sand in a heavy rush of limbs.

"We don't have a choice," she said, panting, and scrambled to her feet. Dirt stuck to her bloody knee. "You have to let me go."

She pulled away and I yelled at her to stop, a long string of negatives pulled from deep in my gut. She took three more steps and the ground collapsed in a perfect circle around her feet. There was a distant *whump* as the dirt hit something solid far below.

Mom shrieked as she fell, high and despairing, and I screamed until I choked on dust. The top of her head, her wild locks of hair, her fingertips—these were the last bits of her to vanish, and then the ground closed back up as if nothing had happened. I tore my nails and bloodied my fingers trying to dig through the hard-packed dirt beneath the first layer of sand.

And when I finally, finally gave up and trudged back to the car—filthy, exhausted, and shivering from the drying sweat and dropping temperature—I stopped short. A woman sat with her back against the front passenger wheel of my mother's SUV. The car door, pinging as it hung open, shielded her from the glare of the setting sun.

She looked over at me, weary and even dirtier than I was. She was white but had a healthy tan under the grime, as if she hadn't spent the last decade underground.

"Hi," she said. I'd seen old photos of her pre-transition, in the albums Gramma had put together before my mom painstakingly pulled off the scrapbook decorations and hid the photos somewhere her sister would never find. She just couldn't quite make herself get rid of them altogether.

"You must be Lucy," I answered. Blood itched as it dripped and my fingertips ached.

Her mouth stretched into a parody of a smile, like her body remembered how to do it, even if she didn't. "Yeah. Your aunt, I think. You're Margaret? Or Maggie?"

"Mar," I said.

We stared at each other, and the fissure in my chest groaned like tectonic plates moving apart. "Well, get in," I said. "I'll drive."

II.

CALLING IT A curse sounds so dramatic, but I sure as hell wasn't going to call it a gift.

Every ten to fifteen years, one of the women in our family disappears, and the one who was gone comes back. Death Valley swallows her whole, then returns its last victim, aged and disoriented. Sometimes they're broken, sometimes they're unmoored, but whatever else, they're never quite the same again.

My grandmother says it's an honor for our family to be part of it all. She says we bring the wildflowers and super blooms to Death Valley, and that it couldn't survive without us.

I couldn't care less. I just wanted it to end.

Ten years in and Mom's SUV was on its last legs, but I'd decided, almost as soon as she left, that I would run it into the ground before I gave it up. These days, the inside lights didn't work and something under the hood made awful grinding noises on cold mornings, but it was beginning to look like it might outlast me.

I sat in the driver's seat in the school lot, engine ticking as it cooled, forehead braced against the steering wheel.

The rain had sputtered in the last twenty minutes and slowed until it felt like we were being spat on from above. I pressed my knuckles to my temples and tried to summon thoughts of the ocean—gray, rolling, and deep as infinity, and then when that didn't work, of green hills covered with whispering trees. Anything but the desert.

The warning bell sounded. I unbuckled my seatbelt, got out of the car, and slammed the door behind me. By the time I reached my classroom, the toes of my shoes had darkened and dampness found my socks. On the way there, the vice principal waved and grinned pointing at her wrist even though she wore no watch.

I held the door for my students, but for a long moment I existed somewhere else: hard-packed dirt, unyielding beneath bare feet, wind heated by the sun until it bites, and air so dry the inside of my nostrils ached.

The desert reached for me, and for a fleeting, horrifying moment, I wanted to reach back.

COUPLE OF YEARS after Mom left, right after my younger brother Kai enlisted, I convinced myself that I could magic away the desert's hold on my family. Because the curse was matrilineal, if I could break my tie to Death Valley, then theoretically no one would be called after me. But everything I read online said that for this sort of magic to work, blood had to be spilled.

I spilled plenty. Nothing changed, and Lucy threatened to commit me if I ever tried something like that again.

"Look," she said while she taped bandages over the gashes in my arms. The waves of her brown hair hung long over her shoulder. "I get that you might want to—that you're feeling a little desperate. But—"

I cut her off, sounding careless even to my own ears. "I'm not cutting and I'm not trying to kill myself. But I *am* going to keep trying to break the curse."

She sighed, but before she could answer, I added, "What do you care, anyway? You've never tried to—"

Save me. I stopped, abruptly realizing I didn't want to hear her response. Not if it meant she really, truly did not care enough.

But Lucy recoiled as though I'd hit her. Her hands dropped from my arms. "I tried," she snapped. "But your mom and I never expected to see our own mother again.

She'd told us nothing, never even *mentioned* Death Valley before it called her, and we had no reason to believe the desert would ever release her. Certainly not that she'd be alive if it ever did. We had no reason to think this would take anyone but her."

But it did affect the rest of us—Lucy in particular, back then. Death Valley didn't just give Gramma back at the end of her time underground. It took Lucy. It stole years of her life as it used her, and more years after it gave her back and she tried to readjust. There was no getting that time back.

I swallowed. Maybe if I'd been a little older when I took my mom out to Death Valley—if I'd been a little less self-absorbed—maybe I could have helped Lucy recover better. Even now, I knew that daily life, the mere fact of existing in our aboveground world, could be a struggle.

"I'm sorry," I said. "I'll be more careful to not hurt myself." It wasn't a promise, but I'd try.

Something complicated passed across her face and landed on skeptical. "So I don't have to worry about this happening again?" she asked, gesturing to the bandages on my arm.

"Long as you don't tell Gramma."

A breath passed, and then she pursed her lips. "Fine."

Mar,

Just checking in. You feeling okay? I counted it out—it'd been exactly ten years since you took Mom out there.

—Kai

I IGNORED DANIELLA until the final bell sounded. Thirty-four other students drained from the room while she leaned back in her chair, legs splayed and arms crossed over her chest. She waited, fuming but quiet, while I answered a few questions.

"You going to write me up?" she asked after everyone had left, eyes narrowed and disdain draped across her shoulders. She was white and had smooth, dark hair that hung to her shoulders and small eyes with shapely eyebrows. She used lip liner and gloss to make her thin lips look bigger, and carried a few more pounds than most of her peers, but they fit her frame well.

I turned away to gather my things. "Maybe," I said over my shoulder. "Should I fail you instead?"

"I didn't plagiarize anything," she said.

"Oh for God's sake," I answered, straightening to glare at her. "What is going on with you?"

Her jaw clenched. "Nothing."

I studied her until she began to fidget.

"What?" she snapped. She couldn't have looked more surly if she tried.

I was seventeen when I drove Mom out. People only expected so much from high school seniors, so I got to skate through the rest of the year. Kai, though, still had two years to go after that and he'd struggled to hold it together.

I set my jacket and purse back down. Daniella watched me approach like she couldn't tell which of us should be more wary of the other. I turned a nearby chair around to face her and sat. "What's actually up, Daniella?"

Her upper lip curled. "Nothing," she said again.

"You got lunch detention for running off in the middle of the day last week," I said. I'd heard so from the vice principal. It was a slap on the wrist, basically.

"What do you care?"

I smelled flowers, daisies and primroses, vibrant and sudden in the back of my throat, but it didn't escape me that I'd said those same words to Lucy, once upon a time. "I just want to know if you're okay."

She crossed her arms over her chest and studied me as I'd done to her. The A/C kicked on with a low, growling hum, but the air remained still. "I don't have to tell you anything," she said.

"That's true." I nodded. "But I'm not looking to be nosy. If you need to vent or someone to talk to, I'm here."

Her forehead creased and she looked away, clearing her throat. "Don't count on it."

Salt crusted over the ground and shimmered in the sun. I squeezed my eyes shut as my mouth filled with dust. Warmth and the petal softness of mariposa lilies and sand verbenas pressed against my arms.

When I opened my eyes, Daniella looked like she knew she'd missed something but wasn't sure what.

"Go home." I blew out a breath. "Just, about the plagiarizing—for Christ's sake, I'm not an idiot. Do your own work. But come to me if you want to talk."

Her expression scrunched, but she didn't say anything as she stood and slung her backpack over one shoulder. She gave me one last suspicious look, then pushed out the door into the overcast afternoon.

IV.

O n New Year's Eve, Lucy got dressed up and went out, while Gramma and I ate Chinese takeout, ducking back and forth from the dining table to the living room until the ball dropped. We blew on cardboard noisemakers until our pit mix Bonnie barked, her tail banging against the side of the coffee table, and then we recorded a video to send to Kai.

The new semester began much as the old had ended—same kids, mostly, and the same classes. It rained the third day back, and the next morning the air felt heavier than it should. I had trouble focusing.

I stopped at a drugstore on the way home one evening and stood in front of an aisle of painkillers, fingers to my temple and eyes closed against the dirty light. All I could think of was rain spattering cold against my skin, raising goose bumps down my arms. Flash floods sweeping down hills to roar across stark mesas and flowers blossoming in the mud as the water drained.

I snagged a few different boxes. Something had to work.

Mar,

The guys loved your video. Yeah, I showed a few of them, get over it. Tell everyone I say hi.

—Kai

❧

EVERY OTHER WEEKEND, weather notwithstanding, the vice principal and I chose a different dog park to meet at and socialize. Susan was closer to Lucy's age than my own. She had two children under the age of thirteen, a moderately friendly ex-husband, and a long-distance girlfriend. I had Gramma, Lucy, Bonnie, and emails and the rare video call with Kai. And a curse, of course.

We had to work around Susan's kids' soccer tournaments and tennis meets, but my recurring weekend responsibilities included grading papers and chauffeuring Gramma to and from her part-time job at a local boutique thrift shop.

Lucy would have to take that job over after I left, I realized, pulling off the main road and into the parking lot. Or maybe, after she'd recuperated from her time underground, my mother would do it.

I parked and twisted around in my seat to face Bonnie, who sat atop an old bedsheet I used to keep the fur and dirt on the back seats to a minimum. The window beside her was smeared with snot from where she'd pressed her nose up against the glass.

"You ready?" I asked, and her tail thumped against the seat. I turned off the car, got out, and opened the back door to leash her and let her jump down.

My mother had been a high school teacher, like me, but she'd given plenty of notice before Death Valley called her. It was the smart thing to do. It kept her coworkers and various administrators from asking awkward questions when she disappeared—she'd already cut ties with most of them.

We needed my paycheck, though. I'd get some extra money

when the district paid out my vacation days, but even so I couldn't fathom staying home every day to wait for the end.

At the dog park entrance, I scanned the faces of the half dozen people there, but none of them were Susan.

I released Bonnie and hung her leash on the chain link fence next to the entrance alongside all the others. A few of the other dogs in the enclosure came over to say hello, but she tucked her tail down and was careful to keep me between her and them.

"Go play, you silly girl," I told her. I turned, and she turned with me. "Go make a friend."

I didn't spend time outside of school with any of my other colleagues. Not on a regular basis. I went to bars for birthdays and brought a dish for our monthly departmental potlucks—I liked everyone well enough, but I didn't search anyone out. If Susan and I hadn't bonded over our dogs, we wouldn't see each other nearly as often.

If I dropped off the face of the earth, she would be the one most likely to question it. She'd be the one who would want to know why I'd quit suddenly, and why I'd done it over email. Was I sick? Did I need help? Was I up for visitors? What about a casserole?

I checked my phone twice more while trying to encourage Bonnie to act like a normal dog, and finally sent Susan a check-in: *Hey, is everything okay?*

About ten minutes more, and I got a response: *So so sorry. In the parking lot, be along shortly.*

I pocketed my phone and kept my attention on Bonnie. She wandered off to pee and then trotted straight back, ignoring the dogs who approached to sniff the wet spot she'd left.

"Go play," I told her again, and she wagged her tail at me.

Then her ears went up, and she bolted past me toward the entrance. I turned to watch as she stood shoulder to shoulder with the dogs she'd been avoiding as Susan unclipped Olive's leash and released her. Olive dropped into a play bow in front of the nearest strange dog and barked twice, then took off at a sprint. The pack, including Bonnie, followed apace.

Susan hung Olive's leash over the perimeter fence, then turned to wave. I waved back and waited as she made her way over.

"Sorry I'm so late," she said. "Work stuff came up."

I made a face. "On a Saturday?"

"There's this woman I know who's trying to get her cousin a spot as a history teacher," Susan said. "He wants to be department chair, I guess? Or maybe she wants it. But he's just way too young."

I tried to keep my expression bland, but Susan saw through it. "David isn't going anywhere for years yet, anyway," she said, waving a hand dismissively. David Harris was the current history chair.

She added, "And frankly, if you started working toward it now, I bet he would even give you his blessing when he does finally retire."

It would still take years, though. Time I didn't have.

For a moment, I tried to envision what it would be like to be free of the desert, but nothing came. I would—what? My entire life was built around my family's connection to Death Valley. What was it people did when released from the shadow of a curse? Travel?

"Oh, Christ," I said, and brought my hand to my forehead, shielding my eyes. I couldn't stand beside Susan, faking normalcy, today. Pretending everything was okay. But I could fake a migraine. I could even pretend it was for a good reason.

"What is it? Did you forget something?" Susan asked, and I gave a minute shake of my head.

"No, I—god, my head is killing me." I grimaced and lifted my other hand to my head. "I've been getting migraines recently," I said, still shielding my face from Susan. "Bad ones, out of nowhere."

I kept my gaze on the dirt at my feet. Bits of crabgrass tried to grow in splotches across the park, but for a moment they were small Russian thistles—the spiky, flowering plant that becomes a tumbleweed when it dies.

The world tilted, and I squeezed my eyes shut. Served me right for trying to deceive one of my only friends.

It would provide good cover in time, though. I didn't personally know anyone who'd had to quit working because their migraines got so bad, but I knew it happened.

"Oh, boy," Susan said. She reached out to steady me with a hand on my shoulder. "I have some acetaminophen in my bag if you haven't taken anything yet. Do you need to go home? Should I drive you?"

"No, I have some in my car," I said, sidestepping the latter two questions, and opened my eyes again. "I think I just need to go home and lie down in a dark room."

Susan placed her hand on my back between my shoulder blades and gave me a nudge in the direction of the entrance gate. "I'll help you grab Bonnie."

Bonnie didn't respond to Susan's calls, but Olive did. Bonnie followed behind her at a gallop, and when I fumbled with her leash, Susan plucked it from my hands and clipped it to Bonnie's collar in one smooth motion.

"There you go," she said, and straightened. She hesitated before handing the leash over. "Are you okay to get to your car? I can leave Olive here for a moment and walk you."

I smiled, but it came out as more of a grimace. "No, thank you. It's early enough that I should be able to get home okay." I stopped, swallowed the guilt down. "Thanks for understanding. I'm sorry about this."

"Don't be silly," Susan said. "It's not a big deal. We'll just try again in two weeks."

V.

THE FOLLOWING WEEK, I sipped cheap wine while Gramma cooked in our little galley kitchen. Bonnie sat leaning against the lower cabinets, tail giving a small wag whenever one of us smiled at her, and Lucy was in her room, pulling herself together before an overnight shift. She worked as a traveling nurse, collecting short term jobs through a temp agency. The long shifts suited her, mostly, though I knew she would have liked to find a more permanent position. That, and maybe something other than overnight work.

The sun hadn't quite set. The window over the sink framed the gathering dusk over the back patio and the wooden fence that had turned from a rusty brown color into something darker, tinted just a little purple, a little more red. It needed repainting.

Lucy appeared from the hallway at the other end of the dining room, hair wet as she applied a hormone patch to the skin just below the waistline of her scrubs. "Almost ready? I have to go soon."

"Yes, yes." Gramma waved Lucy off and pulled a clean wineglass from the cupboard. She handed it to me. "Pour me one when you refill," she said. I did, though she didn't touch it until we sat down to eat. She topped my glass off as we did and then settled into her seat across from me at our little four-person table, picked up years ago at a yard sale in Irvine.

Silverware clinked. A strange, weighted tension had joined us.

"So, Mar," Gramma said. She sat with the same perfect posture she'd tried to impart to the rest of us, cutlery held with graceful fingers. "Are you feeling well?"

Heat twitched like a cat's tail as a fit of childish spite blossomed. I knew where this was going. "Yes, thanks," I said.

"Did you see today's paper?" she prompted.

"Haven't had time."

Lucy paused, knife and fork buried in her chicken breast, juice seeping from the meat. "Mom," she said, half weary and half chastising.

Brilliant red Indian paintbrush intermixed with yellow brittlebrush, and golden prince's plume, pink lantern flowers, white gravel ghost flowers, larkspurs in every color from blue to red: every single one of them bloomed at once in some of the world's saltiest ground, and it was because of us. Because of Gramma, then Lucy, now Mom.

The desert couldn't generate a super bloom on its own, so it used us like batteries. Death Valley took us and what our lives could have been and it used that to make the wildflowers bloom. It needed us.

"There was an interview with a scientist from UCLA," Gramma said. "A climatologist. There's almost certainly going to be an El Niño this winter."

"Mom," Lucy said again.

El Niños meant wet winters and lush springs. It meant spectacular blooms in the deserts, and sometimes, if we were very unlucky, it meant a super bloom in Death Valley. El Niños were the shot over the bow before the desert took the next of us. The stronger the autumn storms, the larger the desert bloom the following spring.

Of course, *storm* was a relative term. A gentle half inch of rain in the desert could cause flash floods and wash away roads.

"I just want to make sure you're braced for what's coming," Gramma said to me. I kept my focus on my plate. "Since you haven't deigned to tell us whether you've begun to hear or see anything out of the ordinary. Have you thought about how you want to handle your departure?"

"I'm not dying, Gramma," I said. My fork clinked against the plate. "I don't need a will."

"You might," Gramma said, so off the cuff that it almost didn't register. "This would be much better if you had a child. A daughter of your own who can call you home when her own time comes."

"*Jesus*, Gramma," I said, and for a moment thought of an old movie we watched together, over and over, after Mom left. *Jesus, Grandpa, what did you read me this thing for?* The memory made me want to cry, which just made me angrier.

"Is that all kids are good for?" I demanded. "To continue the cycle?"

"You know very well that's not what I meant. Do you think I don't love your brother?" she asked. "By your logic I shouldn't. But of course I do. He's my only grandson and I cried more than you did when he deployed."

Heat filled my chest and buzzed in my head like static. I couldn't respond.

"God, Mom, just stop," Lucy said, looking resigned. "This isn't helpful or productive."

Gramma ignored her and tried a different tack. "We are the reason there is life in Death Valley—" she began, but I cut her off.

"That's an exaggeration," I said, and immediately regretted the knee-jerk argument. To my right, Lucy sighed at her plate.

Gramma's jaw jutted out like a mule's, but her voice was even. "It's true, though," she said. "Even if you don't want to hear it, it's true. We are the reason there is life in the desert, and you are the reason we could let your mother go in peace. She loved you just as much as she would have if our family had no connection to the natural world, but it's not just about a mother's love for her children. We—the rest of us—know she'll return because we know who is next. You are your mother's savior, but you don't have one of your own. I just want you to be safe. I want to know you'll be back someday."

"So you're having a crisis of faith, is that it?" I said, on the edge of a snarl.

Gramma paused, so I soldiered forward. "I'm not going to smile and reassure you that everything will be okay. I don't care if you did, or if Lucy did, or if Mom did. I'm not going to."

In the ensuing silence, Lucy rose from her seat, gathering her silverware in one hand and her plate in her other. "I'm out of here," she said. "I'll see you guys tomorrow."

Gramma and I both registered her movements and departure but couldn't bring ourselves to break, to be the first to blink and yield. Lucy huffed and disappeared into the kitchen, a hopeful Bonnie trailing at her heels. A drawer slid open, the clatter of wood on wood, then plastic rattled as Lucy pulled out the containers we used for leftovers.

Gramma gathered herself. "How can you sit here and talk like that?" she demanded.

"I could ask you the same thing," I shot back, but she ignored me.

"This could be the end," she said. "You might never return. Our family will lose our connection to the desert, and all of our *generations* of suffering will have been for *nothing*."

"It's going to end, one way or another," I said. Anger got the best of me. "Kai's not going to have kids, either. There isn't going to be anyone after me."

She stared at me. I glared back, but shock seemed to have tempered her ferocity.

"You don't know that," she said. "You have no idea what Death Valley will do."

IV.

Mar,
Gramma emailed me two nights ago. I take it you decided to let her in on our little secret?
—Kai

Dear Kai,
Sorry, not sorry.
I'm sure she gave you the play by play. It wasn't our most successful evening.
This would be a lot easier if you were here. I feel like I'm fighting everyone at once with no backup.
Love, Mar

Spring crept forward like questing roots. It rained, and for a week everything turned green. Mustard flowers and brittlebrush, bright yellow dots amongst weedy greens, covered the hills and sprouted up in medians along the roads.

Then the Santa Ana winds blew in from the east, one after another. The wind sucked moisture from the air and lip balm began piling up like lost pens after class. Sometimes after work I would turn the lights off, close my eyes, and watch the colors play behind my eyes: pink like hopsage, orange like golden poppies, and purple like asters.

VII.

THE FRONT OFFICE controlled the classrooms' climate systems, so on particularly cold afternoons I propped the door open to let the outside's warmth in. On days without new material or lessons, I'd set the kids a task and lean against the doorframe to sun myself.

In past years, soaking in the warmth hadn't felt quite so satisfying. I wasn't sure if it was in my head, or another symptom from Death Valley that I should be repressing.

On a quiet afternoon of peer reviewing essays, the hum of low voices cracked as Daniella's voice cut across the classroom. My head whipped around as the other students looked up. She sat twisted in her seat, facing the boy sitting behind her. "Daniella?" I asked.

She flushed from the class's attention, her shoulders hunching toward her ears. Then she swallowed and forced them down again. "He keeps trying to shove a pencil down the back of my pants," she said, with an untethered note to her voice.

"No, I didn't," the boy sitting behind her said, instant and automatic, like siblings fighting over half of the back seat.

Outrage bloomed. I snapped my fingers at him and pointed. "Front and center, Aiden." He was a squirrelly, slender guy a little on the short side with angelic blond curls. Not bright, but he would probably manage to pass my class if I didn't strangle him first.

Daniella froze at my tone. She began to sink into herself, so slow and smooth that it was like watching a time-lapse video.

"I didn't do anything," Aiden said, but when I snapped my fingers again he rose and slunk to the front of the room. Bonnie would have caught on faster than he did.

"Bring your things," I said, voice stiff with repressed anger, and he doubled back. Daniella watched him from the corner of her eye, leaning away as he got close again. He glared at her.

I turned to another student, the last to have been separated from her friends at a table in the back of the room. "Congrats, Sylvie, you're out of the hot seat. Go switch with Aiden."

Sylvie's eyes slid to the girl seated to her right, who offered a complicated eyebrow raise and half-shrug. Sylvie wrinkled her nose, but shoved her mechanical pencil above her ear and collected her backpack and spiral notebook.

As Aiden settled himself in his new seat, I stepped close to touch two fingers to the edge of his desk. "You're staying after class," I told him, then looked at Daniella. "You, too. Sorry."

Behind her, Sylvie watched from the corner of her eye, lips twisted in sympathy. Daniella sat rigid in her seat, chin almost to her chest and shoulders raised halfway to her ears, and stared at me like I'd both betrayed and saved her. I had to look away.

Aiden slouched forward, half sprawled over the table. "She's wearing a thong," he muttered, and for a wild moment I was breathless with fury.

At the periphery of my awareness, Death Valley took note and stretched forward. I fought it, struggling to not disappear into myself as I throttled its looming presence back.

"Stand up," I said, and pointed to the corner of the room by the door. "I'm writing you a referral. Go sit on the floor and wait for security."

I inhaled as he obeyed, a short, stuttering breath. Then another. Death Valley subsided, and I was alone in my own head again.

VIII.

Mar,
I am always on your side about this. You're doing the right thing,
and I'm sorry I'm not there to take some of the brunt of it.
—Kai

MY CAR CRUNCHED through holes in the asphalt that had
been filled with gravel, and though there were a fair
number of other cars in the lot, Susan's dark red minivan
was easy to recognize.

The dog park in eastern Escondido that we'd chosen
that day was fenced in, mostly dirt, but with patches of
grass valiantly clinging to life. Susan, sitting on a concrete
picnic table across from the entrance, lifted her arm to
wave. I raised my own hand to acknowledge her and hung
Bonnie's leash on the fence. The park smelled vaguely
of urine, but that wasn't unusual. It didn't rain regularly
enough to clear the reek out.

About a dozen dogs came racing over, tongues hanging
out of their mouths and tails going nuts. Bonnie froze
at the onslaught, then began to thaw. Her tail started
winding up.

I waded through the dusty paws and whipstrong tails to join Susan at the picnic bench. She sat with her back against the concrete table, her legs stretched out in the dirt.

"You found us," she said with a half grin. "I wasn't sure you would."

I sat beside her with a sigh. "We just hit every red between the freeway and here."

Near the center of the enclosure, a little brown mix about two thirds Bonnie's size bowed its front legs and grinned at her. She mimicked the gesture, and then they bolted to the far fence.

"This one is pretty far out," Susan agreed. It had been a good forty-five minute drive northeast for both of us. "I forget sometimes how close you live to school. You have no sense of the struggle the rest of us commuters have to face."

"I take it you're free of the kids this afternoon?" I said.

"As a bird," she agreed. "It's divine. How's your head?"

"The migraines?" I asked. She nodded, and I shrugged one shoulder. This wasn't the first time she'd asked about them. "Could be worse. Could be better, though."

"You been to see a doctor yet?"

I hadn't, of course, but I sighed all the same. "Yeah, for all the good it's done me. Can we talk about something else?"

"Okay," Susan said agreeably. "How's your grandmother doing?"

I hesitated, skimming over my memory of our disagreement to try to reframe it without our curse.

"We're butting heads," I admitted. "And I got an email from my brother about it, so she's been complaining about it to him."

Susan's eyebrows rose. "Classy."

"No, I think I dragged him into it first," I said, and leaned forward to rest my elbows on my knees. "I didn't mean to. I just—we were arguing, and I told her he would agree with me if he was there."

She snorted. "Always a winning strategy. I think it's actually the one Nick tried to use on me when I told him to eat his broccoli. Said his dad would agree that he shouldn't have to."

I was saved from answering as Bonnie broke away from the little brown rescue and came hurtling in, tongue and jowls flopping as she ran. She skidded to a stop in front of me for some enthusiastic pats, then turned to Susan.

"What a good girl you are," Susan cooed, and laughed as the brown mix shoved its nose against her knee. Olive wasn't far behind them. "Yes, both of you are good dogs. Good doggies all around."

Susan may have been a bit of a hardass at school, but a bunch of happy, drooling dogs will soften even the scariest of vice principals.

The dogs jostled against each other for another minute, vying for attention, but then the little brown rescue spun and took off running. Olive turned and hurtled after her. It took Bonnie another moment before she realized she'd been left behind. Susan laughed and quit scratching behind her ears; she held her hands up and said, "Go get 'em! Go on."

When Bonnie chased after Olive and the other dog, I said, "My grandmother's mad that I'm not going to have kids."

Susan went still, and I grimaced. Not the reaction I'd expected.

"Sorry," I muttered. "I shouldn't have said anything."

"No, it's fine," she said, even as the skin between her eyebrows creased in a frown. "You don't want kids?"

"Is it that weird?"

"Well," she said carefully, "not that I'm not glad I won't lose you to maternity leave anytime soon, but—like, kids are off the table entirely?"

I hesitated, then settled on the easy truth of it. "Yes."

She hummed, thinking, then asked, "What if you meet someone you like?"

I shrugged as I debated how much to tell her. She might not be straight, but sometimes even other queer people didn't understand why I was so sure. "I'm aromantic," I said. "I don't want to meet anyone. Not like that, anyway."

"That just means you're not into romantic relationships, right? Or romantic attachments? It doesn't mean no kids," she pointed out.

"Kids are a dealbreaker," I said simply.

"But—" she stopped and grimaced at herself. "Okay. I won't play devil's advocate. Sorry about that."

"That's okay," I said. A smile touched my lips. "I appreciate you saw where you were going with this. And I get that it might be kind of weird for a high school teacher, especially as a woman, to say no to kids of her own. But I'm not interested in continuing my family line."

Understanding shadowed Susan's expression. My refusal had less to do with my personal preferences than some outside impetus, but she was polite enough not to ask for details. "And your grandmother doesn't agree with that decision."

I nodded.

"Well, obviously not," Susan said, half to herself. "Does she know you're aromantic?"

I relaxed enough to sit back against the concrete of the picnic table. "She does, though her reaction was similar to yours. Did you ever think about *not* having kids?"

"Nope," she said. "That was the part I was most excited about when I got married."

We watched our dogs play in comfortable silence, and I thought about telling her the parts I'd held back—that a daughter was considered a necessity in my family, but that my brother agreed with my point of view enough to deny himself a chance at fatherhood.

Susan had taken my side with very little prompting, despite the fact that it wasn't her first inclination. She was a good friend. She deserved better than being ghosted when the desert called.

IX.

Dear Kai,
Do you want kids? Did I strong-arm you into this?
Love, Mar

Mar,
A little. But we made the decision so long ago that I hadn't taken the time to consider the question, so it's been easy enough to shrug and let it be. And I haven't met anyone I might want to start a family with, anyway.

You were right to do it, though. Even if I only had a boy, or boys, they could have had a daughter down the line. This is the only way to be sure it ends with us.
—Kai

AFTER DINNER, GRAMMA sat crocheting in front of the local news, and Lucy slipped out back to smoke. I gave her a few minutes of peace, then dug out a folder of papers I'd printed at school and followed her out.

The screen door groaned as I pushed it open. I felt it tilt, then it fell off its track with a clang and I struggled to catch it. "Goddamnit." I stepped onto the concrete in my bare feet, warmth from the afternoon heat seeping into my skin, and manhandled the door back onto its track.

Lucy sat with her elbows on the foldout card table. She glanced over as I struggled with the screen door but returned her attention to the lighter as she flicked it. "You all right?" she said. The yellow porch light created stark shadows against the ground behind her.

"Peachy," I said, and flopped down on the seat nearest her.

She got the lighter going and held it to the joint dangling from her mouth until orange bloomed at the tip. After exhaling she said, "You know you can talk to either of us about this if you're nervous. Or mad, or whatever. We've both been through it." She paused, then added, "I promise not to lecture you about children."

"I don't want to talk about that," I said. "But I have some other stuff I need help with." I handed her the folder and leaned back in the lawn chair until the plastic creaked.

She flipped through the first few printouts slowly, frowning as she began to skim headlines and diagrams. "What is this?" she asked.

"Our family tree," I said.

The crease between her eyebrows deepened. "Okay," she said, still flipping. "But—why? And where did you find all this?"

I leaned over to see what page she was on. "Public records, mostly. Some genealogy sites, but a lot of the stuff I was looking for had been digitized and put online." I pointed at the heading at the top. "That's Gramma's two younger sisters and their descendants."

Lucy stilled. "No girls," she said, flipping to an earlier page.

"Gramma's oldest sister died in childbirth," I said, to save her some trouble. "It was going to be her first kid, but neither survived. And the second-oldest sister disappears from all public records for thirty years before a doc outside Salinas signs her death certificate. I think she probably just took off after the desert released her. No sign of kids."

"Mom had a brother, too," Lucy said. She glanced at me over the top of the paper, her eyes dark and expression irritated. She was intrigued despite herself. "Uncle Ray. I never met him." Gramma had run off with her high school sweetheart while her own mother was in the desert. She never reconciled with her parents or siblings, so neither Lucy nor my mother had ever met their extended family.

"He's on the last page," I answered. "That's the part I need help with."

She stopped in the middle of shuffling pages, joint dangling from her lips, and stared at me for a long couple of seconds.

"What?" I said.

She shook her head and put the papers down. "This is like the bullshit where you sliced up your arms, isn't it?" she said. "Well, I'm not helping. And I don't think you should be messing with it, either."

"Why not?" I couldn't keep the defensiveness out of my tone.

"Because we consented to this," she said. "Remember? The first of us, or whoever."

"That is not how consent works and you know it," I said, trying not to snap. "I didn't consent. You didn't consent. And just because, supposedly, some long gone ancestor was like, 'Hey, sure, go ahead and imprison me underground for a nice long sentence—'"

Lucy cut me off. "Revoking consent hasn't done you any good, though, has it?"

"That's why I'm trying something different," I said. "I don't have a sister and I'm not going to have kids. Neither will Kai. But Gramma's right about one thing—we have no idea what'll happen after me."

Lucy's expression softened a little, but she still shook her head. "Look," she said, but I cut her off.

"In a perfect world, it would spit me back out and stop taking people. But I might never come back. Or the curse could jump over to the nearest relative in my generation, or retrace the way back to Gramma's aunt's line. I haven't even looked that far back."

"Stop." Lucy pointed her joint at me so I'd know she meant business. "You will come back once you've done your time. The desert will either find someone to replace you, or it won't. None of that is your problem, though. Just enjoy whatever's left."

I shook my head. "What if we can warn whoever might be next?"

"Why would we, though?" she said. "So they can spend the next ten to fifteen years fretting over an impossible thing that might not even happen? Nobody would believe us, anyway."

"What if it's someone with a parent Gramma's age? Or someone with a kid?" I insisted. "They'll want to say goodbye."

She shook her own head and took a slow drag. After exhaling, she said, "The hardest parts are before it happens, when you don't know what to expect, and after, when you come back and have to figure out how the hell to cope. Nobody needs to spend a decade worrying about something that might not happen." For a heartbeat, her eyes went distant.

Lucy took another drag, watching me with pitying eyes. Her exhalation billowed into a cloud, twisting and spreading in the air between us. "Here," she said, and held out her hand.

"Don't tell Gramma what I'm doing with the genealogy," I answered, accepting the joint. "And don't try to stop me, either. Whoever's next deserves to know what's coming."

Her expression shuttered, and she looked away. "It's not the end of the world, you know."

"You already survived it," I countered.

X.

Mar,

Now I'm getting emails from Lucy. Back away from the rabbit hole, please. The curse will end with us. That's why we're doing this. We agreed together, remember?

—Kai

AT THE DAY'S final bell, heads ducked down like a wave and the room filled with the rustling and zip of backpacks.

A suffocating heat smoldered under my skin. I wove between tables and chairs to the thermostat and turned it down four degrees, then returned to the front of the room to flop into my desk chair. All I wanted to do was find a freezer big enough to climb in.

Silence spread across the classroom as the students drained from it. As each one left, the line of Daniella's shoulders relaxed a little bit at a time; she seemed to draw the stillness into herself. It occurred to me that she rarely initiated contact with her classmates—she responded when they spoke, laughed and got carried away with the rest of them when the class turned rowdy, but she didn't have any close friendships. She seemed to like Sylvie, at least.

When it was just her and me left in the room, her eyes flicked up and we regarded each other for a couple of quiet moments.

"I'm going to stay and work on next week's lesson plan," I said, while the room bloomed with desert sage—intoxicating and almost minty. "You can stay, too, if you want."

She swallowed and dropped her gaze again. "Just until my ride's here," she said. The air conditioning kicked on with a dull growl, and she pulled her arms through the sleeves of her jacket. "Thanks."

Dear Kai,

No, see, I've been thinking about it again. We can't be the only family who this has happened to. Setting aside the part where Death Valley is older than humanity, because how the fuck would that even work, what did the desert do before it found us?

There must have been another family. So how did the desert make that leap from them to us? Marriage? Half-siblings, maybe? And don't say the jump was just magic, because even all this bullshit has its own logic.

Love, Mar

I STOOD AT the sink, washing dishes, while Gramma scooped leftover lasagna into a plastic container for Lucy to eat after her shift. The skin of my hands softened and wrinkled under the warm water.

"Have you given any thought to backup plans?" Gramma said. "If Lucy is out of commission, you and I will have to make do."

I frowned at her. "You guys have always said it's impossible to do anything when you're called. Including driving." My mother certainly hadn't been able to.

"It is," Gramma agreed. She tilted the pan to scrape up the last bit of cheese and sauce.

My frown deepened. "So what you mean is, you plan on driving me out there if Lucy can't."

"You're very astute," she said.

Gramma quit driving only a few years after Mom left, and hadn't renewed her license since. I dropped the scrubber to turn and look at her. "No way. If I'm going to be half as out of it as you and Lucy seem to think I'll be, you cannot both drive and deal with me for five or six hours."

She arched an eyebrow at me. "Well, what else are you going to do?"

I huffed and turned back around to the sink. "Call a cab, if I have to. You cannot make that drive."

"I *beg* your pardon," she said, and I schooled my face out of a scowl.

"You may not make the drive, then," I said. "If that makes you feel better. Even if you think you can physically manage it—" And I had my doubts about that, "—I don't want that to be the last time you see me. I don't want you to remember me that way."

"Oh, shit," I said. I already felt kind of like scum for pulling that card, but then Gramma's eyes filled. I stepped away from the sink, but my hands were soapy. Water dripped onto the laminate tile as I dithered between returning to the sink and trying to comfort her. "Please don't cry, Gramma."

She squeezed her eyes and fists closed to sob for one, two breaths, then forced herself calm. She opened her eyes again and said, "I'm supposed to have to say that to you. I'm the one who's going to die first."

I dried my hands on a dishtowel. "I know, I'm sorry. I didn't mean to upset you. But you know that's not how it works with us."

She sagged, hip against the pantry. I held her close, pressing my face into her thinning hair. She smelled like baby powder and her perfume, both layered on too thick.

"I know," she said into my shoulder. "I'm not ready to lose you, though. I'll never be ready for that."

XI.

S OME DOG PARKS were just green open spaces without any perimeter fencing. Some had nowhere to sit, and were only recognizable as a dog park because it was labeled as one online, or—more obviously—because it swarmed with dogs and their people in the workday evening and weekend afternoons.

At nine in the morning, there were only three other dogs at the park in Scripps Ranch. When I set Bonnie loose, the other people and I nodded cordially, but I didn't try to start conversation, and neither did they. I parked myself at the edge of the shade cast by the park's single tree. Standing too close to the trunk was an invitation to smell urine —still, better urine than flowers. Probably.

When Olive came tearing over the crest of the hill separating the park from the parking lot, her tail straight out behind her like a rudder, a laugh like a shot of coffee warmed my chest. Olive didn't see me, but she recognized Bonnie and went bounding up to her, tucking into a play bow at the last possible moment before they collided.

I waved at Susan as she appeared a moment later, and she made her way up from the parking lot. "There's almost no one here," she said, breath a little uneven from the climb. "I thought it would be busier."

I shrugged and accepted a quick hug in greeting. "It's early yet. Everybody's sleeping in."

"Well, Savannah has a soccer game at ten, but her dad is dropping her off, so I can stay until he brings her home afterward."

I cast her a sidelong glance. "You're not going to watch her play?"

Susan rolled her eyes. "My eldest has decided it's embarrassing to have her parents there to cheer for her."

"My brother did that for a while," I said, "though he was younger than Savannah. Turned out he was just stressed by the extra eyes on him. Performance anxiety."

Susan hummed, lips still twisted unhappily. I nudged her gently with my shoulder. "Take a deep breath. She's, what, twelve? Thirteen now?"

"It's going to get worse before it gets better," Susan said grimly, with the knowledge that came from disciplining high schoolers for a living.

I laughed a little, but couldn't help the creaky sort of twinge, not quite a pain, that echoed in my chest. "She's lucky to have you, you know," I said, watching our dogs play. "She might not say it now, but she'll come to her senses after she grows out of being a teenager."

"God, I hope so," Susan answered, and heaved a cleansing sigh. Her eyes slid over to me and then away again. "What about you? How's your aunt?"

"She's fine," I said. "I've been working on a genealogy project that she's all uptight about."

"Some people are like that," she said. "I went through a whole genealogy phase in my twenties, and it drove my mother crazy. The only part she liked was when I asked her for stories about her grandmother and her grandmother's three husbands."

"And what about you?" I asked.

"Do I care about genealogy? Not particularly anymore."

"No," I said, and nudged her shoulder. "What's up with you? What's up with your kids? I haven't gotten a proper update in weeks."

"Oh." She hesitated. "Well."

I blinked. "Oh, shit, something did happen. You're all okay, aren't you?"

"Yeah, everyone's fine. Mostly." She lifted one shoulder in a half shrug. "I'm single again, that's all."

"Oh, no," I said. "I'm sorry."

She shrugged again, this time with both shoulders. "Long distance, you know?"

"It sucks," I said, though I didn't know.

"It sucks," she agreed.

"Do you want to talk about it?"

She shook her head.

Then Bonnie squatted to relieve herself, and I pulled a plastic poop bag out of the back pocket of my jeans. "Be right back."

My jeans swished as I walked, and the grass gave a little beneath my steps. I opened the clean plastic bag around my hand and bent down to pick up Bonnie's deposit, stilling when the thick scent of flowers bloomed. I closed my eyes, fighting against the sudden kick of tears in my throat and eyes.

"Of all places," I muttered to myself.

I swallowed hard and straightened—if I lost my balance while bent over like that, I might end up in a fresh pile—then tied off the bag.

A hawk screeched somewhere out of sight, and I shivered as chills spilled down my shoulders. I searched the sky for a shadow against the bright morning, but didn't see any birds. Hard to tell if I'd imagined it—or rather, if Death Valley had sent it.

When I returned to where she stood waiting, Susan gave me a bemused look. "You okay?"

"Sure," I said, then looked down. I was still carrying a tied-off poop bag. "Ugh. I'll be right back again."

She laughed as I turned away, and when I came back, she asked, "Distracted much? What's going on with you?"

When I didn't answer right away, she prompted me. "Come on. Tell me what's going on. Distract me from my own woes."

I made a face and looked out across the park. "Nothing. I'm fine."

"More than your genealogy project," she guessed. "More migraines?"

"I had another one yesterday, but—well, it's fine. We're all mostly fine at my house," I said, watching the dogs play. In my peripheral vision, I saw the skeptical tilt of her eyebrow, but I continued, "I just—I think my mother's coming home soon."

"Shit," Susan said. "Have you talked to her?"

Telling Susan the truth was out of the question, but everything else I could offer her sounded weak. Like wishful thinking.

"No, it's just a feeling at this point." I blew out a breath. I shouldn't have brought it up. "I know that sounds stupid, but I think things are going to change at home soon. Soonish."

Susan hummed. When I glanced over at her, she'd turned to watch the dogs play.

"Sometimes that's all the warning we get," she said, in a gracious acceptance of what was, in essence, spiritual nonsense. "Do you want to see her again?"

I let out a reflexive laugh but subsided when Susan's expression turned knowing.

"I don't even know," I said, spreading my hands. "It's complicated, dumb as it sounds."

"Naturally," she agreed. "And it's not dumb. She's been gone, what, ten or fifteen years?"

I shrugged. "Closer to eleven, yeah." Her absence still hurt, but the biggest part of it was: "But I don't need her like I did when she left."

I'd needed her so much at seventeen. I couldn't tell how much of my reluctance to accept her return was because it meant my disappearance or from that continuing hurt.

"Of course you don't need her like you did," Susan said tartly. "You're an adult. An intelligent, capable, and well-adjusted one."

Would I get to see her before Death Valley swallowed me? If I was lucky? If I was clever? It seemed unlikely, and a brief glimpse of her wouldn't help things. I probably wouldn't get to touch her or hug her. I wanted an apology, but there wouldn't be even enough time to demand one.

"I've started thinking recently that maybe she didn't want to go quite so much as I'd always assumed."

"How so?" A small frown marred the skin between her eyebrows. I knew, from our previous conversations, that Susan had concluded Mom had walked out. Abandoned me and Kai.

"Like—" I stopped, at a loss. Of course Mom hadn't really wanted to go. I knew that; I'd always known that. But it was only now, on the precipice of my own leaving, that I could maybe understand just how deeply she'd been against it.

I knew now, all the way down to my bones, that she wouldn't have wanted me to be the one to drive her out as the desert called. She wouldn't have wanted me to see Death Valley take her, but by the time it overwhelmed her there had been no more room for anything else. She might have quit her job with time to spare, but she hadn't given me and Kai up. Not willingly.

"It's easier to think of a parent who couldn't—" I stopped, looking for the right words. "She could never live up to my expectations. Parents can't, right, when their kids start to understand that they're human instead of an omniscient, omnipotent barrier against the world's evils?

"I was always destined to lose her, but I'd only just started to understand her as a human, outside of being my mother, you know? And after she left, it was just easier to believe that she hadn't tried hard enough to stay."

"You were always destined to lose her?" Susan repeated, sounding quizzical enough that I realized my mistake and panicked.

"It's just that things were more complicated than I realized at the time," I said lamely.

Olive and Bonnie raced over to say hello. Olive's tail thwacked against my leg, and Bonnie had developed some foam along the sides of her mouth from panting so hard.

Then another dog came hurtling by, and Olive took off running. Bonnie spun after her and kept close to her heels.

At the entrance, a man and his cocker spaniel entered. Bonnie turned toward them, and in a moment it was Olive chasing Bonnie, not the other way around. One of the other dogs growled at the spaniel. The spaniel answered, and soon we were all running to pull our pets out of the melee.

XII.

W HEN I LET myself in after the last day of school, the house breathed with the silence of a single person's existence. Gramma must have taken Bonnie for a walk.

I changed into sweats, made myself some food, and checked my email while fighting off daydreams of the desert.

Then I poked my head into Lucy's room and called her name, keeping my voice low. She grunted, so I left the door cracked and crawled beneath the sheets with her. The air tasted stuffy.

This happened sometimes. She would decline her next gig and quit getting out of bed except to stand in front of the open fridge and try to muster the strength to feed herself. Lucy had meds for it left over from the last time she got depressed, but they took a while to kick in.

She shifted to look at me. Her hair was mussed, her forehead greasy. She'd pulled the blanket up to cover everything below her eyes, open at half-mast.

"Hey," I said, hushed against the unnatural darkness. "Have you eaten?"

She nodded.

"Water?" I said. The blankets shifted as she shrugged, and I propped myself up on my elbow to check her nightstand. Her aluminum water bottle sat half empty.

"I'm sorry," she said. She didn't whisper, but her voice hardly carried at all.

"It's okay," I answered, and tasted sand. "We've all got weird brain chemistry. This isn't your fault."

"Just—" Her eyes watered, but when she blinked they cleared a little. "I wish I could go instead of you." She squeezed her eyes shut. "It's selfish. I'm selfish. I'm sorry. But I just—I'm not like this out there. My head doesn't do this under there, and you don't want to go and—" She broke off again.

It was suddenly easy to match her low tone because I couldn't bear the thought that anyone else might hear me. "I'd trade places with you if I could," I said.

"Me, too," Lucy said. "I miss it. When I'm weak like this. It gives you the most beautiful dreams sometimes."

"You're not weak," I said. "Your brain is fighting you."

We lay facing each other, close enough that I could feel her warm exhales. It was possible, I knew, that she only wanted to go back when she felt like this. I wasn't going to ask, though; I didn't want to know the answer.

"Speaking of brain chemistry, sometimes I think," she said, "now that I'm back..." She stopped, not quite trailing off, and I hummed to encourage her.

"That your mom might have been bipolar. Might be bipolar, I mean," she said.

I stilled. She felt it, of course, felt it as I held my breath and grew fully present and detached from Death Valley. I became my own person again, pushed back into full cognizance by a shiver of alarm that I couldn't help.

"Why are you telling me this now?" Now, when I had one foot out the door?

"I needed to say it out loud to someone other than her," Lucy said. "So that when I suggest a psychiatrist after she comes home, I can say it to her without all my other emotions attached to it. Dawn won't listen if I don't sound objective about it."

We never said her name aloud anymore. Kai and I never called her by her name, of course, but somehow her name had turned into *your mom* over the years.

Lucy watched my face, taking in all the shameful thoughts I couldn't hide fast enough. Her eyes stayed dry, but her expression grew long and unutterably sad.

"I'm sorry," I whispered. "I know it's not something anyone chooses. But it's not just depression, or just anxiety. It's—scary."

If Lucy was well, she'd have scolded me—rightfully so—then come home with all sorts of literature that she'd make me read. She'd done it before, when I struggled to connect with my first autistic student.

But Lucy wasn't well, so she didn't fight me on it.

"Will you talk now?" she asked. "I'm so tired."

"Okay." I rubbed my fingers together and felt Mom's shadow slip away again. Felt petals instead of skin. "Remember I was telling you I hadn't gone through Uncle Ray's family? It turns out his grandson has two kids. I think they're still in elementary school."

"Young," Lucy murmured, eyes closed. "Boys or girls?"

"One of each," I said, and shifted onto my back. The stuffiness was making me start to sweat; I wanted to kick the blankets off, but didn't dare disturb Lucy's cocoon. "Ray's grandson and the grandson's wife, Katarina, divorced two years ago. I can't find the grandson himself, but I don't think that matters."

Lucy opened her eyes. I couldn't read her expression. "Because there's a girl," she said in that same muted tone, further softened beneath the blanket over her nose and mouth. "A daughter. Maybe."

"Yeah. She could be trans. Nonbinary, maybe."

Lucy's fingers appeared and she pulled the blankets farther over her head until only the crown of her head was visible. "You should go meet her," she said. "The woman, the kids."

I frowned and turned my head to look at her. "What, really?"

"You're out of work until August," she said, her voice muffled beneath the sheet. "Now go away, please. I can't—people, anymore. Send Bonnie in when she and Mom get back."

XIV.

Mar,
Maybe Death Valley is sentient. Who cares? Even if it does choose someone after you, it's done with our family. We're safe.
    —Kai

Dear Kai,
We're only safe because our family is ending. There's no one after you and me.
    Love, Mar

Katarina Scorsese—her maiden name, and of no relation to the filmmaker—lived outside Tucson, Arizona, and didn't sound totally convinced of my sanity when I introduced myself over the phone. I told her I was an amateur genealogist, which at that point wasn't even a lie, and that I'd like to meet her and her kids.

I'd be happy to take you guys out to lunch, I told her in a later email. *Or even just coffee, if you'd prefer.*

When she responded, I loaded an overnight bag into Mom's solid old SUV and started driving east on the 8 freeway through the desert. It wasn't Death Valley, which was about a hundred miles north, on the other side of the Joshua Tree and Mojave deserts.

They were all part of the same biosphere, which superseded their boundaries as national and state parks, but Death Valley stood apart even from the rest of its neighbors. Southern California deserts differed in elevation, plant life, and fauna to a certain extent, but they still supported life. Death Valley's elevation was notable, yes—it was the lowest in North America—but it wasn't the elevation that killed off the plants and drove away animals that could survive in the rest of the southern California deserts.

It was the dirt, mixed in and covered with so much salt that even cacti couldn't survive. In some places the salt crust was so thick that it looked like the hardened leavings from a fire extinguisher.

It was also the physical heat that rose to meet the mountaintops and then was pushed down again by wind currents. The heat reached the valley floor, gathered strength until it rose, then was pushed down again, heating further with each iteration. There was nowhere else for it to go.

I almost sympathized. Death Valley pulled us in, held us close, and only let go when there was nothing left to take.

Eventually, the air escaped over the mountains. And eventually, my family rose from the earth—or we had so far. But without the desert's blessing, only the most specific of evolutionary tweaks permitted life within it.

The farther from Death Valley I went, the worse its call became, like it knew I was traveling away from it.

This was why we lived no farther away than San Diego, I guess.

I kept myself sane as I drove by picking landmarks in the distance and watching them grow large and then disappear as I passed them. Hills, rock formations, wind farms. It lulled me. Sand dunes painted with shrinking shadows as the sun approached noon, and hills covered with striations in the distance. A hawk screamed, and then a jackrabbit.

A car horn blared as it sped past on my right, and I jerked back to myself, slamming on the brakes as my car thudded over a string of yellow lane dividers and off the road, into the unpaved and overgrown median. The front of the car dipped, and for a terrifying moment all I could see was the culvert, covered in dead vegetation.

The car slammed over the bottom of the culvert and skidded to a stop with the front wheels on one side and the back on the other. I threw it into park and twisted the keys out of the ignition, then undid my seatbelt with shaking hands and pushed the door open.

I landed hard, and my knees buckled. I fell onto all fours, and for a second I thought I might eat dirt.

"How dare you," I forced out. "How *dare* you."

I sucked in air, panting gulps even while suffocation, in my shaky thoughts, seemed like a real possibility. "You can't have me yet."

Still, it took long minutes until I could climb to my feet; no cars appeared on either side of the road in the meantime, and the relief at being unobserved made my whole body tremble as much as the adrenaline.

I reached for the open car door and ended up banging my thigh against the metal side. It hurt more than it should. I clung to it and tried to focus on staying upright.

Was this how I was destined to live until Death Valley overwhelmed me? Constantly, unrelentingly focused just to stay safe in my own head?

I hauled in a large breath and oriented myself toward Death Valley with only a thought, then screamed at it, shrieking like the hawk it'd just forced on me.

But as my lungs emptied, I sounded more like the rabbit.

XV.

Mar,

Lucy says you're going to Arizona to meet some kid. I get that you think you want to know what happens after the desert—our desert—takes you, but there's literally no way for us to know what Death Valley will do until it happens.

Please don't pull this thread. You're just going to make yourself crazy over it.

—Kai

WITH FOUR-WHEEL DRIVE, I made it back on the road even before highway patrol showed up. Death Valley receded, unchastened, but the rest of the drive was uneventful, even—sort of—tranquil.

I met Katarina and her children at a cafe in a strip mall in Flowing Wells, just north of Tucson. Every time the door opened, the industrial fan bolted above the frame roared to life, blasting the person below. I flinched, scowled, and tried to discreetly fix my ruffled hair.

A woman in the far corner caught my eye and stood. She had staked out two small tables. She sat at one, her back to the wall as she faced the rest of the cafe, and at the other a girl and a boy fussed, half-playing but on the verge of a squabble.

"Mar?" Katarina asked, and beckoned me over.

"Yeah," I answered, and extended my hand. "Hi."

She had a good grip, which I hadn't expected, and a direct gaze. She wore a utilitarian tank top and shorts that almost reached her knees. "This is Cora," she said, pointing to the girl behind her, "and James."

James looked like a tiny Kai. Beneath the last remnants of baby fat, he had the same jawline. The same curls in his hair, and the same quiet suspicion of the outside world. He paused when his mother said his name, but Cora only looked up when she'd lost her brother's attention.

"Hi," she said, shifting to sit on her knees. She wore flip flops and a white martial arts uniform with a yellow belt tied around her waist. Her brown hair caught the sun through the window and threw off shades of auburn.

Death Valley continued to mutter at the back of my attention like the whisper of wind over sand dunes, but nothing actually changed between the drive east and meeting these second cousins of mine. There was no thundering epiphany, no sudden, mountainous realization that Cora was the heir to my family's curse.

Kai was right; I'd fallen down the rabbit hole.

"It's nice to meet you," I said, polite and trying to hide my disappointment. "I'm Mar."

Cora's eyes slid over me. "That's a weird name," she said, ignoring Katarina's hiss to *be polite, Cora*, and turned back to her brother. James watched me for a moment longer, but didn't say anything.

Daniella sometimes wore that same look—that same quiet, acute focus when she thought no one was watching. After a few vague, gentle questions were met with evasion or blank stares, I kept my curiosity to myself.

If I warned Katerina about the curse, it would change their family forever. They'd live beneath the desert's specter, same as I did. She and James would either grow dependent on each other, or spin apart like reversed magnets.

And I loved my brother, but we were tied together by more than blood and affection. We were partners standing against an inevitable tide.

I wasn't going to give the curse that kind of power over James and Cora's relationship.

"I'm sorry," Katarina said. "Sometimes it's like training circus animals. Equally short attention spans."

I smiled. "It's okay. I teach high school, I get how weird kids can be."

She laughed, a short, wry noise, and said, "We'll wait here if you'd like to go order." She'd already bought herself and the kids a drink.

"Thank you. I'll be right back." I pulled my wallet out of my bag and went to order an iced coffee. Even in the A.C., it was too hot for anything else. At the counter, I picked out a pair of cake pops for Cora and James on an impulse, and returned bearing them on a small plate.

Cora clasped her hands together and grinned, and James slid out of his seat to slip in front of her and pick his first. It took Cora a second to realize she would be left with no choice, and when she did, she gave the back of James's head a swift, affronted look.

Katerina also saw the sequence of reactions, and gave Cora a nudge, who scowled at her mother but turned on the charm again as she thanked me.

"You're welcome," I answered. It was a little surreal to watch smaller children behave exactly the way I'd seen some of my students do.

Like Kai, I'd never permitted myself the space to imagine what a family of my own would look like. I couldn't remember a time that I didn't know my mother would eventually leave, and that I would grow up to leave as well. I could never imagine justifying myself to a daughter of my own—she always stood before me, faceless and blurry, expectant and betrayed, her hands loose at her sides as I admitted my selfishness. And if, as Gramma had suggested, I'd had a child just to make sure I'd return from Death Valley one day, I would never have been able to look her in the eye.

Having children of my own had been easy enough to give up, in the grand scheme of things. I'd thought hard about it, made my decision, and now did my best not to dwell.

"So," Katarina said, and I blinked. Tried to refocus as she stood to help James climb back into his chair and handed each of them a coloring book, then gave them each a small box of identical markers. "You guys good?" she asked. James nodded while Cora briefly debated with herself, then relented.

"Good," Katarina said, and turned away to reseat herself. She leaned forward and placed her forearms against the tabletop. "Like I said on the phone, if you're looking for information about Harry's side of the family, I don't have much of anything. The child support is erratic, and we don't talk if we don't have to. It wasn't an amicable break."

"I'm not actually looking for Harry," I said. "But I've been doing all this genealogy stuff and thought, you know, you and your kids are within driving distance—"

Skepticism settled across Katarina's expression, so blatant that I paused and found myself equivocating. I should have practiced in the car before meeting them.

"Well, you're closer than anyone else I found," I amended. "But I mean, Cora and James are family, and you're their mother. That makes you family, too." It was true whether or not Death Valley wanted them, though it felt strange to think of someone outside the curse's reach as family.

Katarina blinked and made a small, pleased sound. "Well, thanks."

I took a sip from my iced coffee. "Are you from Tucson?" I asked. "Originally?"

She nodded. "I grew up here. But Harry didn't. He came out here for school, officially, but also to get away from his family." She made an apologetic face, gauging whether I took offense, and I shrugged it away. "His grandparents had some weird religious thing going on, but he never liked to talk about it."

"I'm not religious," I said, and she flashed a quick grin, relieved she didn't have to ask. "And I think I know which grandparents you're talking about, though I don't know much about them. Are you?"

"Am I what?"

"Religious."

She shrugged. "Lapsed Catholic. I like to think there's, you know, something out there, though. Although—"

I didn't move. My breathing remained steady. "What?"

She swallowed and returned from wherever her thoughts had taken her. "Harry used to talk about how deserts were alive. I always thought he meant metaphorically, but toward the end there…" She trailed off.

I didn't know what to say. "Toward the end?"

"Of our marriage," she said. She glanced toward Cora and James, but they sat engrossed in bartering markers. Cora had two pinks and looked to be aiming for James' purple. He frowned at his cache, doubtful.

"He told me about a family curse," Katarina said, and I inhaled sharply before I could stop myself. I tried to play it off, sighing the breath out and leaning back in my chair, but her eyes narrowed. "You know what I'm talking about, don't you?"

This time I looked over at the kids. Cora opened her coloring book to the back cover and began demonstrating how desirable her black marker was. James' skepticism deepened.

"Yes," I said. "I'm familiar with it."

Katarina's eyebrows drew together, and her mouth thinned into a line. "He told Cora about it, too, right before James was born. He scared her into digging holes all over the backyard. Like in that kid's book."

"*Holes?*"

"That's the one," she said. "He told her I was like the bad guy in that one, the woman with the rattlesnake venom nail polish. That she needed to be good at digging holes because she might end up trapped underground one day."

"That's awful."

"The worst part," Katarina said, watching me carefully, "is that I think he believed it. And I think you do, too."

I looked down at the table. We sat in silence for a long moment, and then Katarina stood. Her chair scraped against the tile as she did, and she placed two fingers on the edge of the table. I'd done the same to Aiden. "We're done here," she said.

I took a deep breath and let it out, then looked up at her. "I'm next," I said. "I have less than a year before Death Valley catches me, maybe under six months. But for what it's worth, I don't think you have to worry about it calling Cora." I couldn't bring myself to declare it like some kind of carnival psychic, but Death Valley had given me no indication one way or another. My intuition said Cora was probably off the hook.

"We're not family," she said, sweeping her kids' markers off their table. James protested, and Cora's eyes bugged out.

"The purple ones are mine! And the pink ones. And the new green one. I need it to make leaves for the flowers."

I stood, too, and grabbed my drink and my purse. "You don't have to go. I will."

She paused and gave me the space I needed to back away from the table. "I don't want my kids anywhere near your family's bull—your family's bunk," she said. "Don't contact me again."

XVI.

F I COULD have faced another six-hour drive, I would have gone straight home. Instead, I booked a motel room on the outskirts of the city, just shy of the nebulous line where the western edge of the city ended and the land reasserted its natural state. There was a strip mall with food options about three blocks away, anchored by a home improvement store.

I let myself into my room and dumped my overnight bag on the floor beside the dresser. Then I flopped onto the bed and stared at the ceiling for a while.

What a mess I'd made.

I closed my eyes, and when I opened them again the light in the room had shifted and dimmed. The clock on the table beside the bed read 6:12.

I sighed and rolled off the bed to shower. The bathroom was dingy but looked mostly clean, and the water pressure was strong. I turned the temperature to lukewarm, then a little colder, and a little colder. Finally, the dial wouldn't turn any further. I stepped directly beneath the spray and pressed one hand to each side of the tile surround to brace myself, then closed my eyes and reached inside myself to where Death Valley muttered at the edge of my consciousness.

At a nudge, the desert roared forward, and I retreated with a jerk and a gasp.

It followed me.

The presence in my mind grew, spreading wings the breadth of a mountain and an appetite as desperate as sleeping seeds for water, until it swooped down at me. Sand whispered across the top of its dunes, and my foot slipped. The world tilted.

Death Valley swallowed as I fell backward, and it was only as my back slammed into the back wall of the shower that I shook free. I slid, hard and uncontrolled, until I hit the bottom of the tub.

Dazed, it took several gasping breaths to orient myself enough to lunge forward on my knees and grab the shower dial. I twisted it until the water cut off, hanging on so I wouldn't collapse. My heart pounded.

"You can't have me," I told it again, still clinging to the shower dial, and almost startled at the sound of my own voice. It came out low and rough, with a growling, defensive undertone.

Death Valley subsided a little at a time. Its inexorable pull crested and waned, tugging at my ankles and sifting the ground away beneath my feet, but I held on. I stayed in the motel. I stayed above ground and I kept hold of my body. My throat tightened and my eyes filled, but I leashed the fear.

What, exactly, had I expected to happen? Death Valley did not bargain. It could not be reasoned with. It took, and took, and took.

I struggled to my feet, one hand on the wall above the dial, and stood dripping until I began to shiver, then straightened and pulled the plastic shower lining open. My stomach growled as I dressed, so I left my pajamas on the bed and put my shorts and blouse back on.

Unthinkable that I had to continue with the business of everyday life after that encounter. That I had no one close enough who would pull me into a hug and pet my hair while I cried.

I sat at the desk chair and unlocked my phone to call Gramma. I turned on the desk lamp against the deepening twilight and paged through the motel's binder of nearby restaurants as the line rang.

It felt like a miracle when she picked up. Like I wasn't alone.

"Hello?" Gramma said. I heard voices in the background and glanced once more at the clock—they were probably watching the news.

"Hi," I answered, and heard an echo of the animal noise I'd made to try to scare Death Valley off. I cleared my throat. "It's me."

"You didn't call when you made it to Arizona," she said. "Not even a text. Are you okay?"

"I'm okay," I said, even as my close calls while driving and in the shower flooded my head. I swallowed and sat back in the chair. She let the pause lengthen, and I blurted out, "I had a scare earlier. I—for a second I thought I'd have to go straight from here to Death Valley."

Alarm tinged her voice. "It wasn't while you were driving, was it?"

Yes. "No. I was in the shower."

"That's still dangerous," she said severely. "You could have fallen and hurt yourself."

I closed my eyes and sighed. "I'm being as safe as I can, Gramma." I would now, at least. No more reaching out; suppression and hypervigilance were the name of the game from here right up until the last moment where I couldn't fight any longer.

"I don't like it," she said. "What if it happens again while you're driving home?"

"It won't. I learned my lesson."

She blew out a sharp breath. "Stop acting like you know everything. You don't."

"Well, I have to risk the drive," I said. "It's not like I can fly home." Driving had its own risks, but being trapped at thirty thousand feet when Death Valley called was too dangerous to even contemplate. "And I can't leave my car out here, anyway."

"I know that," she said, not quite snapping at me. I could hear her frowning.

This was too much. I was heartsore and didn't want to fight. "I'll be home tomorrow, Gramma. I promise."

She sucked her teeth, but didn't tell me not to make promises I had no control over keeping. "Good," she finally said. "Well. What did you think of this woman you met?"

I swallowed and pressed my free hand against my forehead. "It didn't go well. Ray's son didn't treat her well, and he terrified his daughter by making her practice escaping from holes they dug in the backyard. He left, though, so now all they need is a lifetime of therapy."

"It's not a curse," she said.

I swallowed down the accusation that she'd blown right past the mention of child abuse. "You know what I mean."

A sigh gusted down the line, and into the quiet that followed she murmured, "Ray has grandchildren. My god. We've gotten old."

I noted the present tense, but didn't say anything. She knew her little brother had passed more than ten years ago. Heart attack in his mid fifties. Gramma knew before I'd explained my genealogy research, but I still couldn't bring myself to ask how. If she'd reached out to him at some point and chosen not to tell us, that was her decision.

She inhaled, and seemed to gather herself as she did so. "Well," she said again, short and sharp. "What did you think of the girl? The granddaughter?"

I hesitated. "I think she's safe from this. I don't know how to explain that, though. I just—didn't get any response from Death Valley when I saw her."

"You might not, you know," she said. "I spent years quietly fretting over your mother when I should have been worried about Lucy."

"I know," I said softly. She was right—one short meeting, spent mostly chatting with their mother, wasn't sufficient to discern if either of Katarina's kids would be spared the desert because of their gender.

We didn't talk about it anymore, but Gramma had been horrible to Lucy before and for several years after her transition. It took at least as many years after I brought Lucy home for them to reconcile. It helped that Gramma had already spent the time Lucy was underground mulling over the fact that Death Valley had chosen the daughter she refused to acknowledge as her heir. That, and the inescapable proximity of living with Lucy after she returned, forced Gramma to come to terms with her own bad behavior.

And somehow, Lucy forgave her. I still didn't understand how.

I'd stayed out of the whole thing as much as possible. Neither of them would have welcomed my meddling, and my head wasn't screwed on straight then. Kai was the same.

"You know," Gramma said, and sniffed. "You think you know."

I almost smiled. Neither of us knew what to do when the other was being agreeable. I added, "Cora could be nonbinary."

"Hm," she said. "Well. Would you like to talk to Lucy?"

"Sure," I said, as she added in the same breath, "Here she is. Good night, my dear."

"Hey," Lucy said. She spoke slowly, like she'd just woken up or was halfway asleep. "You've been talking shop without shouting at each other. I can't tell you how proud I am."

I snorted. I wanted to confess to her the details of my meeting with Katarina and her kids that Gramma hadn't asked about, but Lucy was still recovering from her depression. "How do you feel?"

"Not well enough to come rescue you if you crash the car on your way home," she said. "So please don't."

"Noted." I hesitated, then added, "Can I ask you something?"

"Sure."

"When did you start feeling Death Valley?"

Lucy was silent for a long moment, but when she spoke she sounded fully awake. "Like how many months beforehand?" she asked, voice pitched low. She knew I wouldn't want Gramma listening in too closely. "The hallucinations? I thought yours started months ago."

I made a negative noise. "No, I mean, did you feel Death Valley before the hallucinations started? Maybe… before you transitioned?"

The voices in the background grew louder in the silence that gathered across the distance between us. Then something rustled on Lucy's end, and she muttered, "Hold on a second." It sounded like she went to another room.

"Okay," she said, sharper than she normally would. "You want to know if I felt Death Valley before Mom was called? Or did you want to know if I felt Death Valley before I started wearing dresses?"

My face warmed with embarrassment. Of course she hadn't.

"The answer to both of those is no. I didn't," she said. "You never felt anything before your mom went, right?"

I pressed the back of my knuckles against my forehead and made an affirmative noise. "I'm sorry. That was really rude and I shouldn't have asked."

"I assume this is about the girl you met today," Lucy said.

"Yeah. I just—I thought—I think she's safe, but that's just intuition." And the fact that Death Valley had ignored her. "Maybe it's just my brain needing closure, or something. But—I don't know. In the moment, I was so sure. "

Lucy sighed and reminded me gently, "We don't really know the details of how this works. The first time any of us managed to prepare was your mom. Before that, she and I had no idea." No idea of the curse before it took Gramma, and no idea that the curse would want someone fresh fifteen years down the line.

I swallowed down my embarrassment and realized my hands begun to shake. Not from emotion—I hadn't eaten anything besides my iced coffee that afternoon. "Thanks. So, everything else at home is going okay?"

"Yeah, we're fine."

"Okay." I waited a beat for her to say anything else, then set the binder of restaurants aside and pushed myself to my feet. "Listen, I'm going to go find some dinner. I'll see you tomorrow, okay? Mid afternoon or early evening."

She hesitated. "Okay. Love you."

"Love you, too."

Outside, the heat hit like a physical wall. I missed the air conditioning right away, but driving three blocks to the strip mall I'd passed on my way in was both a waste of gas and asking for trouble. If Death Valley called again while I was behind the wheel—

I tripped over a crack in the uneven sidewalk. Yeah, I was vigilant. Was driving six hours any more or less dangerous than driving to and from school five days a week? Or to and from Gramma's thrift shop, or the grocery store?

At the strip mall, I followed the closest neon *open* sign into a Mexican place and ordered a few different kinds of tacos, a small plastic bag of homemade tortilla chips dusted with paprika, and extra salsa. I sat in an orange plastic booth facing the parking lot and ate the tacos too quickly; I had to linger over the chips while my stomach settled.

The restaurant faced a large parking lot, at the far end of which stood a home improvement store. Shapes move through and around the loading zone on the near side of the storefront. A man closed the back of a pickup truck, then went around to the driver's side and got in. It pulled away, and a larger commercial pickup truck took its place.

Amid the bustle, another man exited the building, his arms full of garden shovels, and I stilled. He walked around the edge of the pickup area and disappeared into the relative darkness of the parking lot.

A lump of salsa fell off the chip in my hand and splatted on the table. I shoved the chip into my mouth and cast around for a napkin to clean the mess. Could I—

There had to be a reason that bringing a shovel into Death Valley with me wouldn't work. No way could the answer be so simple.

My chest emptied out, and I pushed away the last of my food. I struggled to draw my next breath until I closed my eyes and concentrated.

My next thread to pull. Maybe my last.

I'd have to remember to take the shovel with me when the desert called. That was doable, though; I'd keep it in my car for easy access. The trunk, so Gramma wouldn't see it when I drove her to work at the thrift shop.

I might drop it, though, or the desert might try to take it from me—I had no idea if I could keep a grip on it. Lucy said that Death Valley helped her find the surface at the end when it was releasing her, but we didn't know how or why. It could have been a set of steps that occurred naturally and without any impetus, or the desert might be something approaching sentient. She'd been too out of it to tell the difference.

The shovel would need a handle, then. Something I could slip over my wrist, if possible. It would need to be small and wieldy, but sturdy. I'd have to wake up to use it, of course, but...

From there, my thoughts scattered and I found myself unable to marshal them forward. I had no idea how to overcome a comatose state. And even if I did, would Death Valley really let me out? That same crushing presence that drove me off the road and toppled me in the shower—it would show mercy?

Not likely.

I tied off the bag of chips and shoved them into my purse. Then I stood, cleaned up my mess, and pushed through the door into the Arizona night.

Shovel first. A plan came second.

XVII.

Mar,

I have no idea. Lucid dreaming? But even after waking yourself, you'd still have to get to the surface before you suffocated. Ask Gramma, or maybe Lucy, how far down they were. Or ask them both, and brace yourself for the deeper one.

—Kai

Mar,

Hey, so do you feel like answering me anytime soon? Or have you solved all our family's problems and don't need anyone to talk to anymore?

—Kai

ON THE LAST night of the summer break I lay in bed, thinking in the dark. The blinds shivered against the open window, and the wind in the neighbor's palm trees sounded like rain.

I untangled myself from my bedsheet and got up to open the blinds. The crisp midnight air crept in and out of my open door—we all of us, even Gramma, left our bedroom doors cracked open overnight so Bonnie could check in on us all throughout the night.

I picked up the mostly-clean blue jeans I'd left on the back of my desk chair and tossed them into the hamper. I slid the closet door open gently. I didn't want to wake anyone; this time I was stealing, this last slice of tonight, was for me. All summer, I'd earned approving looks from Gramma—and the pitying ones from Lucy—as I worked on one home improvement project after another: cleaning the track for the back door so it moved smoothly, fixing torn window screens, washing off the front door and porch. I tried to just paint the back fence, but ended up tearing down rotted wood slats and rebuilding large sections of it.

But the new school year started in the morning. I already had my attendance rosters, and I'd arranged and decorated my classroom. There wouldn't be time for more home projects.

I stared at the clothes hanging before me, then sighed and turned instead to the long dresser that sat under the window. I pulled out the casual tank tops and yoga shorts I'd worn on weekends during the summer and placed them, still folded, on top of my unmade bed. I moved on to the casual t-shirts acquired at one event or another—track meets from my own high school days, dog rescue fundraisers, a community Diwali celebration from a few years ago. I piled them alongside the rest of the clothes on my bed.

I went back and forth between the drawers and the closet, purging with a numb coldness that went beyond ruthlessness. Old socks, anything with a hole in it—I ripped the holes larger with the sharp sound of tearing fabric and dropped them on the floor beside Bonnie's bed. Everything else went into one of several growing giveaway piles on my bed.

Hats that I'd owned for years and never worn twice. Heels meant for nights out, ballet flats I'd gotten from a bargain bin. Casual sundresses and dresses for weddings. Skirts just a little too short to be worn outside a party. All belts save the most utilitarian one. Worn-out sweatshirts. Shirts I was never going to fit into again, anyway.

Nail polish. Cheap earbuds. Hair clips and bobby pins. Books I'd never read again. Books I hadn't yet read and now wouldn't have time to. Books I loved that no one else would read. A reusable water bottle. Old birthday cards. Makeup. Cheap jewelry I loved that no one else would wear. A tarot deck I'd never opened. A novelty mug, still in the box. Two pairs of mittens. Four scarves. A folded-up rainbow flag. So many empty journals.

I dropped to the floor with a soft thump. There was so much *stuff*. The detritus of a sloppy life.

This would be my mother's room again soon.

I inhaled deeply, but my breath hitched on the way back out. Hitched, and stuttered, and morphed into a sob. I slapped my hands over my mouth, pressing hard, and squeezed my eyes shut to keep the tears in. I held my breath and scolded myself until the sorrow began to ease.

Then my bedroom door creaked, and I twisted to stare, wide-eyed, horrified at being caught out like this—

Bonnie padded into the room and looked at me. My hands released my mouth, drifted down to the carpet, and as we watched each other her tail lifted and wagged.

"Hello there, baby girl," I said, and held out a hand to her. She stepped forward until she could press her nose into my palm, and I scratched her under the chin and then behind her ears as she stepped closer. "Come here, pretty. What am I going to do without you?"

I knew what she'd do without me. The same sorrow I saw every morning as I left for work. Painful, but eased throughout the day by the distance and dimming memory.

But she didn't have another ten years in her. She'd be gone before I came home.

She sat on the carpet beside me. When I lifted my arm, she leaned in to my side, like she knew how much I needed her, and let me wrap my arm around her.

We stayed like that while the cold breeze filtered in through the open window. When I started to shiver, I kissed the top of her head and stood. "Let's go find something we can bag all this up in," I told her, and we padded out into the dark hallway together.

XVIII.

❧

In September, the true heat of the year hit. The hills blistered, turning brown and yellow, and at home every fan we owned ran nonstop for days. I took a couple of sick days, ostensibly for my migraines, and spent the time grading tests.

Then the week before Halloween, a fight broke out in the corridor outside my classroom.

The voices outside swelled and turned darkly excited. Someone yelled, "Fight!" I looked up from grading papers at my desk.

Teenagers, Jesus Christ. I stood and crossed the room, pushing the door open so hard it banged into a student who'd been too slow to step out of the way. "Ow!"

A crowd had formed. The kids stood in a loose circle, and a few people raised their arms, phones in hand, like they were at a concert. Along the edges, some of them tried to push by their classmates but were waylaid by the gradual act of slowing to watch, like cars on the freeway beside an accident.

Daniella stood across from another student, her shoulders hunched and hackles up. Even from the back, the guy looked vaguely familiar—Aiden.

"Oh, Christ," I said.

She stepped forward and shoved him, putting all her weight behind it. His hand flew out for balance as he fell back a few steps.

"That's enough," I yelled, and pushed my way through the swelling audience of students.

Aiden recovered, then lunged forward. Daniella shifted out of his path and punched him in the side of his chest. It wasn't as effective as her shove, but he still let out an *oof* and stumbled against a nearby planter. The students around me whooped.

Aiden looked up, one hand still spread out against the dirt. "Look, you crazy whore, I don't know what your problem is—"

"You know exactly what my problem is!" Daniella took two quick steps forward. He jerked back, landed on his ass. The weight of his backpack capsized him like a turtle.

For the length of a blink, I recognized her as myself. Alone and surrounded, heartbroken and so angry I could barely think straight. Some things never fully healed.

I stepped between them, facing Daniella with both my hands up. "Knock it off," I said, then to the crowd, "Somebody get security."

Daniella's expression contorted. "Are you kidding me? He—"

I cut her off. "Don't care. You'll be lucky if you aren't expelled for this."

"Bitch, you're fucking crazy, you know that?" Aiden yelled behind me. "It was a compliment. I was being *nice*."

Daniella bristled. "It wasn't and you know it, you disgusting little gutter perv—"

"Jesus, be quiet," I said. I pointed at Aiden as he pushed himself to his feet and snapped my fingers. "You. Come with me. You, too," I said to Daniella. "We're going to find security. They can deal with you two. I have a class to teach."

XIX.

Hi Mar,

Thank you for dealing with Aiden and Daniella yesterday. We've spoken to their parents and decided to suspend them, with the added punishment of two months of after school detention and 100 volunteer hours. (Aiden's prior behavior was taken into account when meting out their punishments.) If they fail to meet either requirement, they'll be expelled.

I know this is a lot to ask, but would you oversee Daniella's after school detention? Aiden's parents insisted they serve their punishments separately, and Daniella specifically asked for you.
—Susan Brenton
VP, Mira Mesa HS

DANIELLA SHOWED UP eight minutes after the final bell, just as I was resigning myself to calling security again. It'd take another fifteen minutes to deal with them, and then another twenty with the staff at the front office. Then paperwork.

I put my forehead down next to the computer keyboard and let out a muffled groan. My back ached and I felt creaky, sort of feverish, almost hungover. I just wanted to go home and lie down in a dark room.

When I looked up, Daniella stood glaring at me from

the open doorway, silhouetted by the light outside. "How long is this gonna take?" she said.

My mouth twisted. "Have a seat."

She dropped into a chair near, but not too near, my desk, while I dug through some papers and found a couple of essay prompts.

"Get some paper out," I said, and placed a printout on the desk in front of her. "You have sixty minutes, pick one and start writing. We can edit it tomorrow."

While she worked, I tried to grade other assignments. I checked my email and stared at the next week's lesson plan. A low-key live wire buzzed beneath my skin, uncomfortable and distracting.

Once, I thought I heard a vulture's raspy hiss. I banged my knee against the desk and winced. Daniella startled.

"Sorry," I said, and her expression melted into a scowl. I waved one hand. "As you were."

At the end of her hour, I called time and gestured for her to bring me her papers.

"Is this what you're going to make me do every day? For two months?" she said.

"Writing and rewriting, yep." I popped my lips on the last word and smiled just to be obnoxious.

She glowered. "They wanted me to sit in silence or— pretend to read, or something."

"This is a punishment," I said, standing to begin packing up my things for the evening, "and you hate writing essays. Also, you need the practice. It's a win-win." I pulled my purse from the desk's bottom drawer, which jangled and clattered as it opened. I'd expected her to bolt the moment she handed the essay over, but she stood there, not quite hovering, not meeting my eye.

"It's supposed to be a punishment for fighting," she said, "but I was just defending myself."

I raised my eyebrows. "He hit you first? Did you tell Ms. Brenton?"

Daniella scowled and gave a half-shake of her head. "I was defending myself in the only way that'd get it through his head that he's not allowed to—to do any of that stuff he does."

"Ah," I said, understanding. "So, then, why now?"

She frowned at her hands.

"Has he been bugging you again?"

She snorted, though her shoulders hung forward and she just looked so *sad*. She'd quit wearing lipgloss. "He bugs everyone. Just saves his *compliments* for some of us."

Too-bright sunshine, blinding and white until I squeezed my eyes closed and felt tears leak along the line of my eyelashes. Heat dripped from my shoulders, down my arms and back like sweat. I breathed in a palpable weight, like smoke given form.

I coughed and clutched the edge of my desk, fingers finding no purchase on the plastic sealing, and tried to—something.

Wind rolled across the salty ground, traveling from miles away. It swept past my small form, insignificant in the midst of the size and strength of the desert. Sand stung my cheeks. I pushed my face into the wind and opened my mouth. I could taste it at the back of my throat.

Death Valley was calling. My entire body was strung tight, muscles clenched like I was bracing for a full-body blow.

For a moment all I could do was try to remember how to breathe.

Everything until this point had been a butterfly's kiss. The realization kicked my heartbeat up a notch.

I opened my eyes. Daniella stood before me, within arm's reach but still outside the invisible line around my desk that most students couldn't bring themselves to cross. She frowned. "Are you all right?"

I blinked at her. "What?" I said, voice rasping against the sand I'd inhaled.

Her forehead creased even further. "Are you. All right," she asked again, and I stared, unable to remember how I should respond.

She swung her backpack around on one shoulder and opened the small outer pocket with a quick zipping noise. "Are you having a stroke?" she said, and pulled her phone out in a single smooth movement. She hadn't even needed to look to locate it. I'd never managed that—I always ended up digging two handed through my purse—and the small, human pang of admiration pulled me back to myself.

"Daniella, stop," I said. She did, fingers paused over the screen. I pressed my knuckles against my temple and tried to figure out what to say. "I'm not having a stroke. I'm not even old enough to have a stroke."

"I don't think that's how it works," she said, but waited, eyebrows raised.

Finally I said, "I'm sick. It's not contagious, but…" I shrugged.

She looked at me, distinctly unimpressed. "Ms. R."

I spread my hands.

"You gonna die?" she asked, expression flat.

"No," I said, and watched the line of her shoulders relax again.

My skin prickled with goose bumps through a sudden sheen of sweat. "I'll see you tomorrow, Daniella," I lied, pushing myself to my feet. I gathered my keys and purse, but left the prep materials for the next day on the desk where anyone could find it. Then I moved toward the door, hands turned out at my wrists for balance.

She trailed behind. "What do you have?"

I leaned against the door and used my hip to push it outward. Pinched the bridge of my nose, squeezed my eyes shut and—

A circling hawk shrieked. I smelled flowers and sweat tickled my eye's inner canthus.

I swallowed and wrenched myself free, stepped outside and let her pass. "That's none of your business, though I appreciate the concern." I turned my back to lock the door, giving her a chance to escape.

She was still there when I turned back around, phone in one hand and arms crossed over her chest.

"Daniella," I said, and sighed. I leaned back against the door and donned my sunglasses. Even the overcast sunlight felt like too much. "Go home."

"You don't look real good," Daniella said instead of leaving.

"Christ," I muttered. Yellow dotted the landscape as far as I could see. Green, swaying in the wind. Purple. White. Petals on my tongue, soft and bitter. Life despite the salt. "Go home, Daniella. I'll see you tomorrow."

"No, really, Ms. R. You got someone I can call, or are you supposed to go to the nurse?"

Distantly, I thought that Lucy would kill me if—I wasn't sure what. I blinked a few times, still tasting flowers, and spat to the side.

Grainy, scorching heat beneath my feet. I dug my toes in, and the dirt gave way.

"I'm not going to the nurse." I grimaced and rummaged through my bag until my fingers found the heavy, slim rectangle that was my phone. I pulled it out, unlocked the screen, and tried to bring up the address book, or the call logs, or something. The wind slipped along the ground, cool from the ocean and so directionally opposite what my skin craved.

Daniella edged nearer and held out her palm. "Can I call somebody for you? Husband? Boyfriend? Girlfriend?"

"Stop fishing." I slumped against the wall and held my phone out. "My aunt. Lucy. She's a nurse. Tell her it's happening."

She gave me a suspicious look and I rolled my eyes, tried to focus on my breathing. We weren't far from the faculty parking lot—closer than we were to the front office, thank God. My colleagues didn't need to see this. Susan especially would have questions I couldn't answer.

A hand touched my shoulder, and I looked up. Daniella frowned down at me. "Nobody's picking up. I left a message, though."

I exhaled and found there was nothing in my lungs but sand. It would fill my nose and throat and I'd choke on it—

I closed my eyes and dropped my head onto my knees. I sort of wanted to throw up. "Shit. Gramma can't drive."

Daniella hesitated. "I got my permit over the summer," she said. Quiet, like she wasn't sure she should be offering.

My thoughts stuttered. She could drive, everybody knew where Death Valley was, more or less—maybe not, probably not—but I certainly knew. I could guide her. I shouldn't be driving, but she could still get me there before I lost my mind. Probably.

Except that she was my student. I couldn't drive her out to the middle of Death Valley and leave her there with no explanation beyond what she witnessed. That was worse than what my mother had done to me.

I couldn't actually call a cab, though.

"My gramma," I said. "She'll be under *G*. Call her. I need you to drive me to her."

XX.

I KEPT MY eyes closed as Daniella drove. I had trouble tracking the passing world outside, and it made me queasy to try.

The glass warmed my forehead, and I pushed myself up against the door to press as much of myself as possible against it.

"Hey," Daniella said. I cracked an eye open to look at her watching me with wide, sort-of-alarmed eyes, one hand hovering over my shoulder. "You're being weird. Are you okay?"

"Hands on the wheel," I muttered. "Just listen to the GPS lady, it's fine."

❧

THE CAR JOLTED as we took a turn a little too close and clipped the curb. I cracked my eyes open in time to watch the hospital that Lucy was working at slip around the corner and out of view.

Daniella chewed her bottom lip as she eased us over a speed bump and into a parking garage.

"I need you to call Lucy again," I said. My voice came out rough and low, like I was coming down with the flu. How had Daniella known where to go? Had I given her directions?

"Please shut up, Ms. R., this is hard enough as it is."
Slowly, she eased into a parking spot and uttered a tiny,
victorious curse. My thumb clicked the seatbelt free and
I opened the door, stumbled out. The seatbelt wrapped
around my elbow and I swung back, nearly collided with
the car.

The driver's side door slammed shut a half second after,
and Daniella appeared at my elbow. "Fuck, slow down."

"Language." I couldn't quite straighten for fear of
upchucking all over my nice work shoes. If they made
it back home before I did, they definitely belonged in a
giveaway bag. "Where are we? Call Lucy again. Tell her
she's gotta come now. Family emergency."

"No shit," she muttered, and placed her hand on the
outside of my elbow to gently guide me. "Get back in the
car, Ms. R."

"Call Lucy again," I repeated, and hunched over
further.

"I did," she said. "Seriously, Ms. R. They'll definitely
expel me if I get my teacher killed on an unapproved field
trip."

"I don't think that's how it works," I said, but climbed
back in the car, this time into the back seat, and stretched
out on my side. Speaking to the ceiling, I added, "But
since this is a fully unapproved field trip, you might as well
call me Mar."

XXI.

Mar,

I've been too chicken to say it, but you're not answering your emails. I hope to hell I'm panicking for nothing.

Anyway: if I had to pick between you and Mom, you'd win. Please just hold on a little longer. I want to see you before you go.

I hope you get this, at least. I love you.

—Kai

I HEARD VOICES and opened my eyes. Lucy had opened the door by my feet and stood turned away, speaking in an underwater hum to someone standing behind her. When I blinked, she stood at the near side of the car and peered down at me. I meant to say something reassuring, but if I opened my mouth the only thing that'd escape would be nonsense about deserts and goodbyes.

I closed my eyes instead. Opened them, and we were on the freeway. I couldn't tell which one. Daniella was still driving and my head lay pillowed on Lucy's thigh. Someone had wrapped a seatbelt around my middle.

"Kai," I said. My voice came out as a croak.

Lucy twisted to peer down at me. Her lips moved.

"I hate this," I answered, unable to draw enough breath to speak, and closed my eyes again.

THERE IS NO rainstorm on earth like the one that descends on Death Valley after it swallows one of us.

I remembered the drive home with Lucy. Clouds gathered on the horizon almost the moment we got into my mother's SUV. I had twisted the ignition, put the car into gear, and eased us back onto the road. The wind kicked up while I accelerated, and by the time we hit seventy, the force of it pulled against my grip on the steering wheel. Blood and dust smeared everywhere I touched.

The rain had started all at once. It boomed like thunder against the windshield, drops so fat and violent they splattered the view into kaleidoscopic darkness broken only by our headlights.

Lucy had been curled up in the front passenger seat, knees against her chest and twisting sideways to fit. She'd pulled at the seatbelt until the cross-chest strap cradled her head against the window, then closed her eyes.

I remember I couldn't tell if she was breathing, but being too scared to pull over and check.

WE STOPPED FOR gas outside Barstow. Lucy handed over a credit card and Daniella got out of the car, pocketing her cell phone with a deft movement. The wind pushed her hair into her face, and it tasted like the desert.

The inside of my nostrils ached. There would be no sign of rain for a while still, not until we arrived at least.

"You gotta send her home," I rasped.

Lucy looked down at me. Her hand settled in my hair and she stroked, gently. "She wouldn't go," she said, and for a vertiginous moment her words didn't match up with her mouth. "And it's not like we can leave her by the side of the road now." The look on her face said she'd seriously considered it.

"Phone," I said.

Her eyebrows drew together, but she leaned forward and I heard something heavy clatter in the center console. "Here," she said, and wrapped my palm around the back of it. I felt the corner against the meat of my thumb and I squeezed it tight.

"I already talked to Mom," she said.

"Mom?" Then I remembered. Gramma. "Oh. Good."

Kai I'm Surry I'm sorry I'm sorry I live you

XXII.

I JOLTED OUT OF half-awareness as the road changed. We dropped from fresh asphalt onto concrete—older and less uniform, with its double-yellow lines bleached pale by the sun. I lay alone in the back seat, a red hoodie balled up and smushed beneath my head. Lucy sat in the front passenger seat. Daniella still drove.

I pushed myself up, one hand braced against the back of Lucy's seat. "Roll the windows down," I croaked. My throat hurt like I'd been breathing in Santa Ana winds thick with pollen and other detritus.

Daniella glanced over her shoulder at me, expression taut. "Are you crazy?" she said. "Don't answer that. I'm not turning the A.C. off."

Lucy reached forward and twisted the knob. "Sorry, Daniella," she said. "It's important. The windows, please."

Daniella grimaced, but her hand went to the controls at her left elbow.

I leaned so far out the window that my seatbelt pulled me up short with a yank. I gripped the windowsill with both hands, rubber and metal pressing against my palms.

"Here," I yelled, and pulled myself back into the car so fast I almost bashed the back of my head against the frame. I threw my hand out the window and pointed to the right. "Turn here."

"What?" Daniella threw a harried glance at Lucy. "What about the doctor you said we were going to see—"

"Just do it," Lucy said tightly, and Daniella, caught in the hysteric edge between excitement and panic, hit the brakes too hard and turned directly into the scrub brush.

Twigs cracked against the car and flew in all directions. One shot through the window and hit my cheek, just below my eye; after a moment it began to itch. I raised my fingers to my face and they came away bloody.

The view didn't look any different after the turn except that the road began to shrink into the distance. Scrub, tumbleweeds, and incongruously large dead branches dotted the landscape. The ground stretched out, flat and mostly level enough to see to the base of the mountains.

After a while, something in my chest loosened. "Stop," I said. "Here, stop! This is it."

"Gently," Lucy said to Daniella as she eased on the brake.

I barely noticed. I couldn't concentrate.

Daniella shifted the car into park and yanked the hand brake into position. She stared at it all for a moment, then slumped forward over the steering wheel and sighed.

I scrabbled for the door handle and lurched out, squinting into the overcast light. The wind gusted, full of chaparral and petrichor.

There was something important that hovered in the back of my head, some knowledge separate from the sand clawing its way up through the back of my throat—

I kicked off my work shoes and plain gray socks. The topmost layer of dirt was made of gritty, irregular grains that hurt the bottom of my feet.

Lucy dropped out of the rumbling car. "Mar," she said.

Daniella turned the car off and slammed the driver's side door shut behind her. She watched me from across the hood with some strange mixture of confusion and disquiet, and not a little trepidation. "There's no hospital, is there?" she asked. "There's nothing out here at all. We're not even on the right road to Vegas. What the hell are we doing here, Ms. R.?" Fatigue strained the faint lines on her face, and for a moment I could picture what she'd look like when I returned in ten or fifteen years.

The desert wind ruffled her hair and pushed a few strands across her face, and the blinding clarity I'd spent the last year searching for settled over my chest. When I returned, I wouldn't find her. She was next.

Horror bloomed in my throat like a sob. I'd driven to Arizona on the vague hope that if I could just lay eyes on whoever was next, something inside me would sit up and I'd just know. But my heir—my daughter—wasn't a blood relative.

Didn't mean she wasn't mine, though.

Another gust of wind brought the scent of rain, and a shudder ripped through me. Daniella frowned and looked me over. Barefoot but still in my teacher clothes, with my hair pinned up in a haphazard bun and my too-crisp-for-comfort blouse. "Ms. R.," she said. "You're sick, right? Come get back in the car." She looked at Lucy for help.

"You're right," Lucy told her. "There is no hospital. I don't even know if there's a doctor out here. She's cursed, not sick."

There was a beat. "What," Daniella said. "Wait, what?"

I emptied my lungs and used the motion to center myself, just for a moment. I could keep it together for another minute. "Daniella," I said. I thought of my mother, sitting in the dirt beside her car just as Lucy had. I still had small white scars on my fingertips from trying to dig her free. "Daniella, you're next. You have to tell my brother. His name is Kai. He'll help you."

The wind blew stronger and I stumbled a little. I could barely keep my attention on her, on either of them. I pulled out my hair tie, wrapped it around my wrist. I'd need it when I returned, probably. If it didn't disintegrate underground. Wasn't there something else I was supposed to take with me?

"Daniella," I said again, and tripped as I turned away. "God, I'm sorry. You have to go now. It's going to flood. It's going to be bad this time."

"Mar, wait," Lucy yelled.

I halted, but I couldn't quite turn back around. The wind shifted, and dust kicked over my bare feet. The heat from the afternoon sun seeped up through my soles.

"I can't," I said, but Lucy lurched forward and grabbed me around the waist.

"I'll miss you," she said. Her hair smelled like my lemongrass shampoo. "I'm so sorry. Be brave. I love you."

"I love you, too," I said. I felt Lucy pull back and gesture behind her. "You have to tell Kai—"

"I will," she promised. "Don't worry, I'll tell him."

"Ms. R.?" Daniella said. She slipped up alongside my right arm and circled her hand around my wrist, watching me with those same wary eyes from the classroom. "Mar."

"Daniella," I said again. My heart sighed with relief, and I released Lucy. "Daniella, I'm so sorry. I didn't know."

"Where are you going?" she burst out. "We're in the middle of the fucking desert and you're—going somewhere! There's nowhere to go."

"You need to go now," I said. "We both have to go." My vision blurred, and I laughed once. It came out sounding wet, like I'd been crying. "You have to let me go now." Mother to daughter. God, I hated mine sometimes. She didn't deserve it, but I did.

The breath punched out of me, and I staggered away from them, gasping.

Beneath my feet, the ground softened, then turned slippery and shifted. It felt like standing at a cliff's edge, trying to back up fast enough to stay on solid ground as it crumbled.

Eyes wide, I looked back. Daniella met my gaze as the ground dropped a few inches and my arms flew out to the sides for balance. Her expression twisted as confusion warred with terror. Then the ground opened up beneath me, sliding away in a perfect circle from my feet. I fell.

Daniella screamed. In that scream I heard the echo of my own, and my mother's, and my aunt's, and their mother's, and her mother's, stretching all the way back to one terrified, heartbroken woman who took her own raving mother, in pain and out of her mind, to an unmarked place in the desert, and watched the ground swallow her whole.

ACKNOWLEDGEMENTS

THANKS FIRST GO to dave, editor and publisher extraordinaire, who saw Mar's potential, pulled her story out of the slush pile, and helped me fall in love with her again. I went into this whole publishing thing with no small amount of trepidation, but you were awesome at every turn.

And thank you to K.R. Mayer for the *beautiful* cover! It's a delight to work with you.

Thirdly, thank you to my beloved Clarion class, the Awkward Robots. The very first (incomplete) draft of *Death Valley Blooms* raised its hand as we were putting together The Yellow Volume anthology, and it was the thoughtful feedback from Deborah Bailey and Dan McMinn in particular that led me to think that there might be something worth mining a little deeper than our anthology timeline permitted.

Thank you also to everyone at Stonecoast who helped nurture this novella from a second draft into something I am so very proud of. This includes Theodora Goss, who acted as an advisor for two (!) semesters and whose brainpower regularly floored both me and her other students; Nancy Holder, who held my hand through my third semester project and who was so kind when I wrote an awful, anachronistic short story about Lucy; David Anthony Durham, who was likewise extremely forgiving as I stumbled through my second semester; and James Patrick Kelly, for leading that first critique workshop on the Bowdoin campus the summer of 2017. And of course, thank you to everyone in that critique group: Savannah Hughes, Rhiannon J. Taylor, Kyle Derek Long, Eric Schultz, and Marcus LiBrizzi.

(A confession: when you all asked if I had written the end, if I knew how everything would wrap up, the "oh, definitely," I gave was *brazenly* untrue. It blew my mind that all five of you immediately agreed that Daniella was Mar's heir, and I suspect I'd still be floundering without your insights.)

Thank you to Christina, Maggie, Britty, and Ragan. I'm so lucky to have known all of you for so many years. And a special thank you to Maggie for your name—there is no other name on the planet that I could tend to with such love as I did for my Mar, and that stems directly from our years together on THW—and to Christina, who understood my glee when I reported this story had made several other friends cry. You always understand, which is no small thing.

Gabi and Laura, who helped me through *so* many decision crises that needed immediate answers. Thank you, thank you, thank you for helping me keep my head above water while also offering candid and constructive opinions at the drop of a hat. I wouldn't have gotten through the yearslong process of publishing without either of you, and I hope we keep texting all day, every day, forever.

Also, even though it's unlikely she'll see this, I am deeply grateful to Kelly Link and how encouraging she has always been to baby writers. Years ago at a book signing, when I shyly told her I'd just gotten a short story acceptance, she burst out with such excitement that I felt seen and even a little important. And when I waffle about how weird to make my fiction, I reread some of her absolutely unhinged short stories to remind myself that if I don't weave my own unique brand of insanity into my work, no one will get to see it. And the world needs all of our weirdest ideas.

Finally, to my family: Mom and Dad, you've supported my writing since the very, very beginning, and I would never have made it as far as I have without you. And Gavin—yes, Mar loves her brother as much as I love you.

ABOUT THE AUTHOR

S.M. Mack is a 2019 MFA recipient in popular fiction from USM Stonecoast, the 2017 first place winner of the Katherine Patterson Prize for Young Adult Writing, and a Clarion 2012 grad. Her short fiction has been published in *Fireside Fiction*, *Vine Leaves Literary Journal*'s "Best of 2015" anthology, and the Clarion class of 2012's seven Rainbow Anthologies, among others. Her novella *Death Valley Blooms* is part of Neon Hemlock's 2025 Novella Series.

Find her online at @whatsmacksaid on Bluesky, @what_smacksaid on Instagram, or sign up for her monthly author newsletter on her website at whatsmacksaid.com.

ABOUT THE PRESS

Neon Hemlock is a Washington, DC-based small press publishing speculative fiction, rad zines, and queer chapbooks. Publishers Weekly once called us "the apex of queer speculative fiction publishing" and we're still beaming. Learn more about us at neonhemlock.com and on social medias at @neonhemlock.